ONE CHANCE ENCOUNTER

Joy M. Lilley

Absolute Author Publishing House, New Orleans, LA

Absolute Author
Publishing House

One Chance Encounter
Copyright 2020 by Joy M. Lilley
All Rights Reserved

Publisher: Absolute Author Publishing House
Editor: Dr. Melissa Caudle
Interior Design: Dr. Melissa Caudle
Cover Designer: Rebecacovers

Library of Congress In-Publication-Data

Joy M. Lilley /*One Chance Encounter*

    c. pm.

    One Chance Encounter/Lilley, Joy, M.

ISBN: 978-1-951028-45-9

Other Books by Joy M. Lilley

Strawberry Moon
Figs, Vines & Roses
The Liberty Bodice
Time's Pendulum Swings Again

Dedication

To all the women who have searched for love everlasting.

Acknowledgement

I wish to acknowledge Jean Mead, author without whose advice I would not have completed this book and my editor Dr. Melissa Caudle for her skill and expertise.

Table of Contents

Chapter One

Summer 2010

Close to Moyra's sixtieth birthday; the first contact was made.

As a child, Moyra had a difficult upbringing, surviving tuberculosis and still at a young age caring for her dying mother until the end. Her life made more arduous as she also had a considerable amount of responsibility for two siblings.

Her adult life also brought difficulties, with a marriage that failed to give her the happiness and love she sought.

This day she had a weird sensation that something was going to happen. It was an itch that perpetually pestered her.

As she looked out of her bedroom window, the birds' songs drifted near as they chirped away to each other. The day was fortuitously warm and sunny, and the light ethereal being early June in the Surrey countryside.

Moyra lived close to the farm where she had worked for the last fifteen years.

What she had known and cared about before had gone and was a dim and distant memory.

After her difficult childhood and adolescence, Moyra wanted once again to have someone to care about and someone who would care for her. Being a mature lady when she entered married life, she imagined such caring could be found — thus giving her a chance at happiness and companionship. She had been wronged and soon realised her husband was a self-centred tyrant and a control freak.

Her working life involved employment at a nature reserve, come farm, in the depths of the countryside. She'd been an assistant helper there. It was a job she loved and had no wish to change. She found it to be a refuge and a place of escape, allowing her the privilege of communication without argument.

This day Moyra was clearing out the paddock and stables close to the main country road where deer, antelopes, cows, and sheep freely roamed. The early summer westerly breeze was warm and comforting. The birds she loved to hear sang as if in competition with one another. The smaller, gentler, songbirds did not stay around long when the seagulls came swooping and wheeling in making their presence felt as they screeched behind the neighbouring farmer's plough, who ploughed unusually late this year.

She looked up from her chores in the barn where she was replacing straw for the horses when she heard the roar of a car's engine passing nearby. There, as she looked across the meadow from where she stood, a large grey limousine was parked by the wire fencing in clear sight between the hedgerows. It was a huge car, with the hood down making a show and gleaming the sun's warmth. As she moved closer, she noticed the cream leather looking, grand interior, and a handsome man sitting in the driver's seat. Her eyesight, not as good as it should be and in need of cataract surgery, didn't stop her from shuddering slightly as the driver left his car and began to walk toward where she had been shovelling and removing a pile of freshly excreted dung. It still wafted a dreadful stink with steam rising. Her hands were entirely covered in shuttle joys of this work had never bothered her until today as she saw this handsome middle-aged man jump the intervening fence and almost run in her direction.

She attempted to brush her long, dark hair from her face, realising that she had left muck in her dark brown locks. She felt out of bounds to be anywhere near another human being, especially one looking like he did.

Who is it? She thought! *Is it; yes, it is, it is Tom, Tom Ursuline.*

After what seemed like an eternity, he smiled and said, "Hello, I wonder if you could direct me to a place around here called Shere? It's a small village. I seem to be lost. I'm not used to being here in England."

She was speechless as he took a step closer to where she stood; the silence between them was deafening and unnerved Moyra.

She was sure it was him; however, a modicum of doubt crept in. Then, she summoned up the courage stuttering her reply. "You, you need to follow this road until you come to a crossroads, then take a left turn, carry on for about three miles and then it should be right in front of you and clearly marked."

Being dumbstruck and glued to the spot, afraid to move, she weakly uttered, "You, you are who I think you are, aren't you?"

"I think I very well may be," came the response in a deep, soft, gorgeous, American accent. His eyes, those eyes, they were transfixed on her face and did not move as he flashed an impish, dazzling smile and an unmovable stare renowned for when talking to you.

"Thank you so much, have you seen any of my films?"

"Yes, yes," she uttered. "All of them."

"And I take it you are a fan of mine?"

Her mind quickly flashed back to the last film she'd seen him in, just in case he asked her about any of them. "I loved all your films. I don't think I've missed one of them. And yes, indeed, I am a fan," she said fidgeting from one foot to the other. All this time he was looking at Moyra, making her more uneasy by the second.

"Yes, I'm so lucky to be able to work in a job I love; and enjoy all that goes with it. Is this where you live?" He enquired, still smiling at her with those wide eyes.

"Yes, yes, It's Crown Yard Farm in Surrey, Kent South England."

"What is your name?"

"It's Moyra, Moyra French."

"Well, Moyra French, watch and wait as there will be something nice coming in your direction after I get back to the States. Thanks for your help. Have a nice day, Moyra, Moyra French, goodbye."

Then he walked away, turning back and waving to her when he reached his limousine.

Then he was gone from her life as quickly as he had come into it.

***

Spring 1959

In a two up, two down terraced house in Chesterfield, a large market town in the borough of Derbyshire rented by her parents, was where Moyra and her siblings were raised. Her younger sister Jane, by three years, and an older brother Frank, by one year.

The place was small and had a box room in which Frank slept. There was only room for a camp bed and one small locker you could only squeeze around. There wasn't any window and only a tiny lamp for any light. So, unless the hatch-like door was kept open, you could not see a thing. There was an outside toilet which was freezing in winter, and it had a wooden seat. This Moyra considered a luxury as it kept her bottom warm even though the rest of you froze. For toilet paper, hung on a string were newspaper bits cut into squares to wipe you clean. The old tin bath used once a week and by the whole family using the same water, always hung on the outside wall in the back yard next to the toilet. They took turns to go first, and there were always arguments about whom that was going to be.

As there were only two bedrooms and the box room, Frank had to keep all his belongings and clothes in the cupboard under the stairs. A kitchen come dining room and a small sitting room, known as the parlour in which housed a two-seater, threadbare dirty couch that barely fitted along one wall with a second-hand sideboard on the opposite wall.

Their mother, Gladys, kept all her crockery in this sideboard and the cutlery in two drawers at the top. The home had no carpets; the flooring was made up of lino cut-outs. Her ailing mother managed to buy them cheaply from the local ironmongers. A few rugs made by mum graced the kitchen and sitting room floors, these were made up with bits and pieces of re-used cloth woven into a canvas base. The coal fires found in every room were only lit on the coldest days of winter, and even when they were alight, ice frozen on the inside windows.

Families living in this area were as poor as church mice and all were desperately struggling to make ends meet and survive as best they could. The children's father worked in the steel industry, eleven miles away in Sheffield.

The place was known as the Black Country because of the coal industry and poverty thereabouts.

From an early age, Moyra's health had been doggedly grim. She had a constant cough that drove those closest to her to leave the room, keen to escape the fracas. Her siblings would watch her cough her heart up, go blue in the face, and then tut before clamouring to the nearest bolt hole. She'd been seeing the doctor for months now and they were no closer to finding out what was wrong than when her visits began.

God had given her a weak chest, her mother frequently announced. As a child, she regularly needed to be dosed with oral antibiotics, Vick Vapor Rub on her chest, and other unmentionable concoctions.

Moyra always remembered it this way. Every winter going from one chest problem to another, she was subjected to all the antibiotics recently available in the fifties, after War World II in the United Kingdom.

"The child has a chest weakness that will be hard to keep under control, and any improvement is likely to be slow. Perhaps we should send her away to one of the London hospitals; maybe they can come up with a solution. Make sure she always wears a vest, mother," the doctor exclaimed.

She didn't; however, she did wear the liberty bodice, a newly designed garment to help keep the winter cold at bay. A frightful thing it was, with rubber buttons down the front and her mother made her wear it or a bigger version of it until she was the age of fifteen. It would be passed to her younger sister when she'd outgrown the wretched thing.

It seemed to all the family that day after day was spent in trying to improve Moyra's health. She was made to stay in one of the London chest hospitals for ten days that seemed like a lifetime to a small child. No parents or siblings could visit as Tuberculosis was suspected. After what seemed like years of blood tests-xrays, and God knows what else was on offer at the time, the diagnosis was eventually made. "She has tuberculosis of the lungs Mother and needs to be in a sanatorium," the doctor proclaimed.

What on earth was a sanatorium? I'd heard that people who were very ill were sometimes sent to these places for treatment and many didn't return home. Moyra shivered at the thought.

Her mother swiftly carted her back home on the new red bus, and she kept blowing her nose. Moyra even thought she saw a tear or two dribble down her mother's cheek.

"Are you all right, Mum?" She asked.

"Yes child, I'm fine, come along don't dawdle, I've to get tea ready for your Dad, he'll be home soon."

With that remark, she grabbed her daughter's hand, and they moved along at a feisty pace, so much so that Moyra was panting for breath when she almost fell over. She was not feeling so well that day having a bit of a fever, and her mother made it clear she must get to bed as soon as they arrived home, adding she would call her when tea was ready. Her rest was short-lived as she was awoken by the loudest bang coming from the kitchen. Voices were raised and her mother was crying. She was unable to get back to sleep after the drama. She tossed and turned and hoped her sleep would return. Eventually, she gave in and got up. When she made her way downstairs, the noise had ceased. Her sister was home from school. "School, gosh!" She sighed. *How long was it since I'd been to school? I missed my friends and had not seen many of them in ages.*

Moyra enquired as to where the noise had come from. She was told by Ann, "Well, it wasn't me, so don't go blaming me for it and go and tell Mum."

Then given an explanation she didn't believe, she later discovered it was her mother dropping the cast iron bathtub on the floor as she brought it into the kitchen for the weekly bath in front of the kitchen stove; the warmest place in the house. This was an epiphany when for the first time, she realised just how weak her mother was becoming.

At the age of twelve, Moyra was sent to be treated in a sanatorium. She was so frightened; it was like her life changed from colour to black and white for a young girl who'd known nothing but sickness the whole of her young life. She was now to have one of the worst experiences of all. She arrived holding her mother's hand tightly. The building stood way out in the countryside. They were shown along a dark and dingy hospital corridor which led to a similarly dark and dingy Florence Nightingale type ward. Another long corridor of a ward with smartly made beds lined along either side of the walls. The nurse's station comprised a desk and a lamp in the middle of the long ward. A few chairs were around the desk for staff to write their reports and rest their legs when not attending to patients. Their uniforms were stiffly starched collars, cuffs, belts, and hats gracing a white and green striped strong cotton dress.

She was the only child among so many grown-ups. Some were nursed indoors and some on the verandas, out in the cold all year round. That was the treatment back then. They were told that fresh air was the best treatment for the disease and informed they would be kept warm and cosy. These poor souls stayed out in the fresh air no matter how cold the winters were.

Moyra's home was in this place for almost two years, after which the doctors declared she was cured and able to be released back home.

***

The whole family cried on her arrival back into the fold, including her.

It was a short-lived expression of love and affection because even in her state of recovery and slow progress, she was still expected to do a considerable amount of fetching and carrying. Helping raise the children was an unspoken requirement.

This was expected because her mother was not herself in the rudest health, and it was to become Moyra's lot to take and fetch her siblings to and from school each day. On return, it was her role to prepare the tea and be a general factotum.

She tried her hardest to help her Mother as she felt sorry for her after her husband had left the family. She had one of those debilitating conditions, some dystrophy she thought it was called. There were so many diseases around in the forties and fifties in Britain.

It was now the late fifties and the country still trying to repair from the devastation and loss caused by War World II. Progress was slow, money was tight and building materials scarce.

Moyra was now thirteen, and on top of the other expectations of someone still a child she was required to undertake her school work at home. She was not allowed back into her school for another year. That was the ruling in those days. Even though it was believed she was no longer infectious. Her homework was picked up every school day morning by one of her school friends from class and who lived in the next street to Moyra. Her friend had to talk to Moyra a room away as she was not allowed to mix with other young people during this year of purgatory. The fear was that she might pass the disease on to them.

"Mind you, that didn't seem to apply when it came to care for my sister and brother," she muttered on a regular basis.

She missed her friends from school who were also not allowed to visit. She missed the chatter and games and the company. The situation and isolation were beginning to get her down, and she became quite depressed.

***

The struggling family grew up without a father figure, as he, being the useless creature, he was, decided to leave them all for pastures new. She apparently came in the shape of a hussy, from the nearby town, who wore fancy clothes, high-heeled shoes, and plastered on make-up, which included thick, bright red lipstick.

Moyra's depressed state found it all a bit much, coping with her sister and brother, especially when they didn't behave, and she found it impossible to keep them under control. She often took herself to her room to escape the fracas.

Her mother, weakening week by week, tried her hardest to support her daughter in all that confronted her. She always had kind things to say and gave Moyra as much encouragement as she could.

One day when everything got too much, and she felt unable to cope any more, her mother caught Moyra crying at the sink where she was doing the washing up after having made tea for them all. The other two had been moaning and making unkind remarks about their sister's efforts in cooking and she began to lose control. The tears just ran down her cheeks dropping into the washing-up bowl. It was the only way she seemed able to release the tension. Her Mother hobbled over to where Moyra stood, put her arms around her daughter and held her tightly in her arthritic hands, for a moment or two.

"Don't do that my sweetie, it's just not worth it!"

It worked as Moyra found the next few months passed without drama, and the family appeared to buckle down and accept their lot in life. There was a considerable financial hardship to contend with and they all needed to find ways to be thrifty making do and mending like so many other families at the time.

The siblings grew up a great deal during that summer and when winter finally arrived, they were well prepared. They had worked hard to harvest all they could from the small garden they managed to tend and raise a considerable amount of produce.

Moyra and her mother bottled as much fruit as they could find Kilner jars to put it in. The children all went out picking the blackberries and sloes to make jam and gin. There was no way she could afford to buy a bottle of gin. The children had such fun dressing up warm and going out together on a cold winter's night, laughing and chattering and playing ghosts to scare poor Ann. It was possible to make one bottle of gin from the sloes found on the hedgerows in the surrounding countryside.

After the children were asleep in their beds, mother, enjoyed the only treat the woman ever allowed herself.

Chapter Two

When Moyra reached the age of sixteen, she had the opportunity to go and work for a family in need of help to raise their children. She was more than qualified to do the job. However, she failed in her school exams and left without gaining any qualifications. Her illness had negatively impacted on her educational abilities, which upset her mother tremendously as she blamed herself for this deficit.

The chance of a job came one day as she was leaving the school gates a lady one Mrs. Reynolds who lived nearby, on the right side of the town tracks, asked her.

"How old are you now, Missy?"

"I'm in desperate need of someone to help me rear these children of mine. I cannot do a thing with them, and they're driving me mad. How would you like to come and be a live-in caregiver for the children? You would be paid well and all your board and lodging free?"

She, of course, was more than tempted by this offer being the grand gesture it was. However, Moyra realised that Mrs. Reynolds was unaware of how sick her mother was and that her siblings seemed still to be reliant on her for their food and washing.

Her brother was by now itching to leave home and make a life for himself away from the family. This worried Moyra as she felt that although he was a useless item in the home, he was at least someone she could talk to and share a few thoughts and moments with when the going got tough.

She decided not to mention any of it to her mother, knowing how upset and distressed she'd be at the thought of losing her stalwart helper, and her son, who made no secret of the fact of his desire to leave home.

Both Moyra and her mother were aware of the sacrifices being made. Nonetheless, she decided to stay home and continue as she had become so familiar with cooking and cleaning and caring for her ailing mother, that she feared the consequences of removing herself from the situation.

She attended to her mother's every need, ensuring her cleanliness was maintained and paramount. Even though this task was becoming more and more difficult until the day she could no longer get her mother into the mega shower, they saved for and managed to purchase.

So, becoming bed bound, Moyra became adept at blanket bathing, which took a great deal of time and energy to maintain, both for Mother and Moyra. One major bone of contention came in the guise of hair washing. She resisted as long as possible, saying, "It doesn't need doing today, you only did it the other day. It's all right; just leave me alone in peace."

Then Moyra would get annoyed, and only then did her mother give in and allow the hair-washing to take place.

This process was exceedingly difficult when the patient was bed bound. Moyra needed to pull the bed away from the wall with her mother in it. Then do the washing at the head end of the bed with her Mother complaining and shouting out during the procedure. She called her daughter all the names under the sun throughout.

The main change in Moyra's sorry life was the fact she no longer attended school. She began to dream of what her life might have been had it taken a different path to the one she had been destined for. She daydreamed about the exams she likely would have attained and the career she'd have probably could have carved out for herself.

She did all she could to fill her thoughts otherwise as she was aware of dreaming over what might have been never brought fulfilment refusing to let these thoughts take over her life and told herself enough already. Self-pity was no attribute.

The years passed, her brother had left long since, and her sister grew up and left home.

Moyra's Mother died at the tender age of fifty-five. She had nursed her at home until the end and was totally dependent on her now. Her siblings occasionally came back home for a visit; however the visits were always short-lived and usually ended in a row breaking out especially with her sister who determined that she should not be giving up her life and that their mother needed to be cared for in a home.

"You're killing yourself like this Sis; you have your own life to lead. After all, you have cared for her since we were little. Now it's your time."

"How old are you now, Moyra?"

"You know how old I am; you don't need to ask me that."

Being glad to see her sister leave, Moyra decided that she may have had a point and that perhaps she should take a bit more care of herself.

Then she would be laden with guilty feelings, look over to her Mother's lovely face, and become overwhelmed by the need to care for her.

So, life continued as it always did until the day her mother died.

Moyra's life was turned upside down, and her grief took over all other emotions. She cried until no more tears came.

Chapter Three

Moyra looked at herself in the mirror, something she'd not done in a long time, seriously, and instead of looking the twenty years she was, she looked much older. The stress and toil of the last few years had aged her to the extent of non recognition.

She knew she should do something about it and decided to have her hair done at the local hairdresser and then buy herself some make-up. She made the appointment the day before the funeral took place. She did not want the rest of her sparse and distant family to see her looking like the wreck of the Hesperus.

She had no trouble finding black clothes as most of her wardrobe was full of black and dark brown dower clothing.

After the trip to get her hair done, it looked lovely, styled into a kind of a bob, which was easy to do with her thick, silky brown hair. The style suited her, with the round-shaped face she possessed. It had been ages since she had applied any make-up. She wasn't sure how to do it. So, she went along to one of the big stores in town and asked if they would talk her through what she needed to do. They succeeded, for when her sister and brother arrived at the house, they were both astonished to see the changes in her appearance from the last time they had seen her.

"Hi, Sis, wow, you look fab; you really do! Glad to see you are taking care of yourself at last," Frank uttered as he took hold of his sister, pulling her off the ground and swinging her around. He didn't appear to show any remorse for losing his mother; however, her sister did a bit of saying the right words. Moyra could not help but think that it may have been to placate her.

The funeral was short and sweet — the day dark and grey with a slight drizzle. A few distant relatives came and with the three siblings made up a congregation of just ten, excluding the Vicar. He gave a kindly address about Gladys having gained the information from Moyra. She had decided to invite everyone back to the house and with the help of her friend Iris, had conjured up a few tasty finger buffet eats. Coffee and tea were readily available, and she had no time to think about what was happening. That was until everyone except for her brother left. It was then that she broke down and wept on his shoulder for what seemed like hours not the minutes it was.

"There, there, Sis, don't let on so." He took a long deep breath. "You are now free to get on with your own life. You've had so little of that for the past years, now have you?" He shifted his weight from one foot to the other as he pursed his lips before flopping onto the settee.

"I know, but I'm going to miss her so much." Her eyes flushed with tears. "She has been such a huge part of my life for so long," she uttered as she retrieved her hanky from her dress pocket and blew her nose, putting it back into the pocket. "Any way Frank, enough of me, tell me about what you are up to these days." She eased next to him, sitting several inches away and faced him.

"You know me, never in the same place for long." His eyes averted hers as a bead of sweat formed on his upper lip.

"What about the girl you told me about the last time you came down?" She crossed her arms.

"Oh, she's long gone. We weren't as good together as I thought we'd be. Anyhow she's out the picture now, and I'm on the lookout for a new model." His left brow quickly lifted as if to anticipate a new beautiful woman in his life.

"I hope you find one soon, don't you want to settle down?" Moyra suggested.

"Tell me what your plans are Moyra." He scratched his chin. "Have you thought any more about what you want to do in life or are you planning to get married and start a family?"

"Chance of that would be a fine old thing now, wouldn't it, where have I had any time to find myself a bloke." She huffed with exasperation.

A thin-lipped grin formed. "You're looking good; now love, it won't be too long before you find a nice chap to settle down with. How old are you now Moyra?" Frank stood up from the settee they'd occupied for the last half-hour. He kept fidgeting from one foot to the other and looking at his watch.

It appeared he had cramped or something. After what he thought was a suitable time to spend with his sister, Frank made his excuses to leave promising to keep an eye on her to make sure all was well.

His passing shot was to ask if she intended to stay in the house or to sell it. "It might be a good idea to sell, and you could find somewhere smaller and more manageable to live. After all, we could all do with the extra cash you know love, would you like me to get the place valued?" and with that remark, he left.

Following the initial shock of it all, Moyra knew she needed to think about getting a job. Her search was rewarded when she found a suitable role as a care assistant in the local nursing home. The pay was appalling, and some of the patients were demanding. However, she continued to work there, diligently for a further four years.

After having been encouraged by senior staff, at the home, to think about a career in nursing, she seemed like a natural fit; she sought out that schooling with a certain hesitancy.

Having given the matter considerable thought, she decided that she may turn out to be quite a good nurse. She'd enjoyed her time in caring for older patients, on the whole, and the prospect of nursing in a variety of other specialities appealed to her immensely.

She needed to do quite a bit of research before she could think about applying and realised that to become a trained registered nurse, she would need to attain several qualifications.

She asked at the local hospital about what she needed to do to train as a nurse and was somewhat alarmed on learning she needed to go to night school to be able to enter a school of nursing because the requirements were at least five times for the General Certificate of Education.

The pursuit of her intended career began. She needed to study hard every day for the next two years, eventually succeeding in attaining every exam undertaken.

***

When she entered nursing school, she felt somewhat out of place. All the students in her class were still in their teens and Moyra was now twenty-six. She got fed up with explaining to her colleagues the reasons for entering her training as late as she had.

"You could be in a senior position by now, in charge of everything," she was told by some of the newest recruits.

She did aspire to develop her skills in her chosen career and eventually be promoted to a senior position. She was aware of her somewhat ambitious personality, one that would lead her to greater glory in any line of work she chose for herself. She also pondered from which parent that could possibly have come!

After the three-year training course, she settled on becoming a surgical nurse as this was her favoured specialty. She had discovered this when her training took the students into the various types of nursing available. From the care of the elderly, children, adult or mental health or accident and emergency, along with orthopaedic specialities, she made her decision.

She enjoyed nursing adults best of all, having a flair for the calling, and looked forward to going to work each day and coming home exhausted, cooking a bite to eat and eating it alone. Her loneliness was beginning to take a greater hold on her life these days, particularly in the cold, wet, winter months of the Pennines.

The family was no longer close enough for regular contact. They also didn't keep in touch with Moyra, and when they did their constant nagging advice and necessity to sell the family home, would upset her so much that she'd come off the telephone in a worse state than when she went onto it.

"You should sell up and get a smaller place, a flat, or something similar. Go get a dog or a cat, have a bit of company, you must be so fed up being on your own, Sis?"

Soon after that last phone call, her brother decided England was not for him and so still being single took himself almost 12,000 miles away to New Zealand and he loved it. He had found work on a sheep farm and soon joined in with the community comprising mostly of men. Her sister and the family, she now possessed, moved further up north to where her husband's work had taken them. To some extent, she felt relieved about this, as the pressure of constant reminders of why she should sell up and why she had not yet found herself a husband diminished, but it increased the loneliness tenfold and now felt seriously alone.

This was the reason she loved going to work each day as there she found like-minded, caring people to talk to daily. The patients also played a significant role in dulling the self-pity that being home alone, she was inclined to wallow in.

One piece of advice given freely by her brother led to the purchase of Henry, the most lovable golden retriever puppy you ever could meet. The day arrived when Henry came home. He was a beautiful golden retriever puppy of eight weeks, whose capers of which were unthinkable to her. It did not take long for her to get used to them and the acceptance that this was the way a puppy behaved. She soon learned that a puppy must be kept in a cage for a time. She disliked the idea of that, but life would have been impossible without a certain amount of restraint and her home would have ended up a wreck. On Henry's arrival, Moyra took two weeks of her annual leave to help him settle in. She hadn't put much thought into the care and attention he would need when she was working. Fortune came in the guise of Hazel, her next-door neighbour who had always longed for a dog of her own but was never allowed to have one. Her partner did not like animals and insisted that there would be no pets other than him in their relationship.

When Hazel's fellow left for work each day, she dashed to Moyra's house to let Henry out for his pee. Then off they would go on a lengthy walk. This relationship Hazel considered being of far greater value than the one at home with her partner.

He soon grew and became less unruly, in fact, he was a very good dog and a strong bond developed between him and Moyra. They needed each other so much. The greeting given when she arrived home after whichever long shift she had been assigned, was both dog and humans delight of the day. He made such a fuss with jumping up and whining as a puppy dog does; this was so compelling and disarming to Moyra.

As he grew, she loved him more and more and now could not imagine her life without this sweet boy in it.

After preparing food for Henry and herself later, they would sit together on the long, comfortable settee cuddling up and watching the television.

All this love and attention from another creature got Moyra to thinking that for the first time in her life, maybe she should look for a human companion to share all the love she appeared to hold in her heart.

***

Moyra had quickly risen the greasy pole in the nursing hierarchy and was on the verge of attending the interview for the position of the recently vacated post of Junior Surgical Ward Sister.

If she were fortunate enough to get the job, she would work regular hours with no weekend or night shifts. This would be far more convenient to help stop the current lack of any social life available and allow her more time to spend with her furry best friend.

She became totally dependent on the goodwill of Hazel; and as such, the two became close. Hazel told her, "I would do the job for free as I love him as much as you do."

"I will not hear of such a thing; you will have a pay packet every week my friend, for, without your help, I'd not be able to have a pet at all. I'm so grateful to you for all you do, and I know how much Henry loves you."

The current situation meant that shift work was inclusive of many unsocial hours expected. That came with the job of a Staff Nurse. You just had to fit work and home life around it. Others managed to achieve it with families and often little ones in the mix.

She felt deep inside that with all this love to give, just maybe some of it should be given to a real live human partner as well. Someone, she could share everything with and who would speak to her. She deduced she was a much happier individual after Henry came into her life, and she would hug him and spend much of her free time stroking and grooming his long light white and ginger coat.

Winter had just morphed into spring, Moyra's favourite time of the year.

She and Henry would spend hours going for long walks down to the woods, which he absolutely loved. He would chase the squirrels until they ran up a tree and into the rising sap, and then turn and look for her as if for approval, then with a noisy flurry, he'd dash straight into the muddy pond and come out stinking of whatever rotted in the putrid water.

This day she had much to think about and so stayed out until it was almost dark and turning colder. She pulled her coat tightly around her neck and fetched her gloves from the coat pocket. She needed to blow her nose as it had started to run down her face, almost reaching her mouth. The job offer had her wondering if she should attend the interview or stay where she was happily working, at least for most of the time as a staff nurse. Part of her wanted to remain in the sanctity of a familiar setting. If she were to succeed in securing the posting, her life would change considerably, and the comfort zone would be lost.

She knew of the major commitment in running a ward of thirty patients and a considerable workforce that went with it all relying on her and dependent on her for the last little drop of knowledge and common sense she was expected to have. She doubted herself at that moment thinking she may be making a big mistake. Was she capable of such responsibility?

By now, Moyra had reached the grand age of thirty-two, and if she was going to make this move, she would be wise to make it sooner than later. Nursing at this level was usually sought in the thirties, and it was not getting any easier; the population was living longer than previously, and many nurses were currently leaving in their droves as the job was proving to be too much. There were so many demands and they could get better-paid work elsewhere.

Many had young families to take care of and trying to juggle that with the demands of a nursing career was more than could many were able to cope with. She knew of several good nurses who were being always encouraged to do further training in this and that.

"Go off and get a higher degree, that way you will be able to go to the top of the nursing tree."

Many were neither capable nor willing to do any of it. For many, it was not the right time to even be considering such a change of direction, mostly due to their family life in one way or another.

Life was good for Moyra; it had never been better. In fact, she wondered how on God's green earth did she manage to run a home and care for her mother the many years she had.

She now had her Henry for company, which had improved her lot immensely. She had no one else to answer to apart from at work. She relished the fact that she could now make her own decisions without the anguish of having to ask permission from anyone.

She recalled her mother always having to beg steal or borrow to be able to make ends meet and always having to ask her father for money or permission to buy anything. Poor Jane; she always had to get on with my hand-me-downs. She didn't remember her sister ever having new garments to wear. The clothes she did wear came from jumble sales. These were regular events in the nearby town.

One day Moyra witnessed her father lash out at her mother alarmingly, smashing his clenched fists across her head. She fell against the stove and burnt her hands badly. He failed to see how close by Moyra stood. Mum needed daily dressings and walked to the doctor every day for weeks after the event for the required treatment to her burns. She never let on to the family how the accident happened, always wearing white cotton gloves, saying to the three children that she had fallen onto the stove and acquired the burns.

Moyra never let on that she saw what happened, and she also never forgave him for doing that to her mum.

***

Moyra was glad when he finally walked out. However, she was well aware that it had broken her mother's heart and wondered how on earth she could feel such pain at the loss of a man who treated her like she hardly existed and who beat her on more than one occasion? She never complained to the children about what he did. They were all better off without him.

From that day forward, she vowed to herself that no man would ever get away with treating her in this way and considered the possibility that she may be better off in her single marital status.

Chapter Four

The day arrived for the Junior Post interview; she went with such fear and trepidation finding it hard to believe she'd agreed to put herself under such a strain, but she had.

It was to be held at the hospital where she worked. She arrived right on time, one of her assets was always to be a good time keeper and if considered being accepted for the post, then her high standards would be expected from those she worked alongside.

Her standards had always been the highest, and she had no time for those who didn't follow her good example.

Four people sat on the interviewing panel.

Being ushered into the interview room was dreadful. It was late in the afternoon, and the light beginning to fade. The whole place was dark and dingy just like Charles Dickens' 'Bleak house.' No smile or reassuring conversation greeted her as she was ushered over to a seat in front of the stern-looking foursome. She couldn't help but think the whole set up was a bit over the top for a nursing post.

As she sat down, she realised she was confronted by none less than Matron Dehaviland, an awesome looking woman who was the only familiarity and had a ghastly reputation that preceded her. She apparently could be as wintry as the Arctic air as it pours over the northern plains from the North Pole. The other Senior Nursing personal was made up of the Night sister, Home sister and the general Surgical Ward sister. Moyra tried hard to stay calm and keep still but found the whole set up the most unnatural experience ever.

Matron was an imposing woman of almost six feet, perhaps not quite that tall but much taller than Moyra. Neither bad nor good looking, she fell somewhere in between with shape eyes missing nothing darting from left to right like a frightened animal. She also processed a prominent pointed nose.

This was a foreboding place, and Moyra concentrated hard to prevent herself from making some feeble excuse and bolting from the room.

She didn't; something made her stay. She took deep breaths before deciding to smile, which helped her relax more, and the interviewing team appeared to relax more as a consequence; indeed, they all, in turn, smiled back.

And off they went.

Questions followed one after the other. Although well prepared, she realised by some of the questionings that she may not have prepared quite well enough.

It went on indefensibly, and by the time the end came, she was utterly exhausted, considering that perhaps they were too.

"Well, Nurse French, do you have any questions for us?

"Yes, I'd like to know what the starting pay is going to be."

"That's easily sorted, just pop along to Human Resources and they will sort it all out for you!"

She did feel that they too should have been better prepared and at least known the answer to her one question.

She went to get up from the chair and was relieved when she did as she could feel the blood rushing back into her buttocks; it was a hard and comfortless seat. That may well have been a deliberate move. A voice boomed out at such a level she was taken aback and told in no uncertain tone that they hadn't finished yet.

She quickly found herself sat back down on the unrelenting chair, almost knocking it over in the process.

"One last question if you don't mind?" Miss locker, the night sister, stated.

"You must have heard about the new system which is being muted all over the country about something called internal rotation. What do you think about the concept? I would like your views, please, nurse."

Damn it, she thought. She knew she would have to act excited and approvingly of this new concept, but she didn't feel that way. She just wanted a nine-to-five job that didn't involve the unsocial hours she had known for so long.

On the walk home, her thoughts were gloomy and took her into concern about this bold move she'd made, and she now had doubts. Was she cut out for the heavy responsibilities of such a senior position? Would she be able to handle it? And if this bloody new system came into play, she would be no better off than as she was at present. *Maybe, just maybe,* she thought, *I'd be better off staying where I was.*

The news came through to say she had been successful in attaining the position of Junior Ward Sister for the male surgical ward. She hesitated to open the letter. She was so confused about what to do. She felt that if she didn't take the job, she might even have to leave the profession, and that is precisely what she did.

Without regret, she handed in her notice offering to work for the next three months so that a replacement could be found. She was aware of how difficult it was to recruit nurses. It would also give her time to look for another job.

Chapter Five

L ife took a strange turn in the guise of a neighbour. The neighbour was a single gentleman, or at least that's how he came across to Moyra. The only connections between them so far had been a hello or good morning as she was taking Henry for his early morning walk.

This particular day, spring had taken on a new dimension and the sap was rising.

Moyra loved this time of a year and noticed all the new shoots and buds pushing their way out into the world. The Winter had taken a toll on everyone as the snow and significant icy conditions had lasted from January until the first week in March.

As she was getting ready to leave the house with Henry, who wore his brand new coat designed to keep the cold and wind out, she opened the front door, peeped out to make sure it hadn't started raining as that was in the forecast, when her neighbour, dressed in his Barber Mac and heavy boots, passed by.

"Well, hello, young lady, this is early for you to be going out."

"I need to walk the dog before I go to work. That won't be for much longer, though, as I'm leaving at the end of the month."

"Oh, that's not good news. I was under the impression that you loved your work. You always seem to be happy and smiling when we pass."

"No, I have had enough of it. It's darn hard work, and there is such a shortage of nurses right now, making it even harder for those still there. They are even going abroad to try to recruit them and I don't spend enough time with Henry having to rely on Hazel to take care of him when I'm working all the hours under the sun."

"Have you found another job, or are you still searching?"

"No, not yet, there's still time. I don't want to be out of work. I can't afford to be."

"I hope you find something soon, Miss, I must go now, or I shall be late. Bye for now."

And with that, he was off. There had been no introductions between the two of them and Moyra wondered about him, was there a wife? If so, she had never seen her.

Later that week, after getting back from her walk with Henry, she thought about catching the bus into town and going to the job seekers' office and see if anything she fancied had come in. When she arrived, she was disappointed to find a long queue in front of her. She then decided it would be better to do the shopping she needed and come back later. Things were not much better after a couple of hours so she decided she'd wait. An hour and a half later, she was called to a booth. The rotund fellow seated behind the glass appeared to be a decent enough chap with a smiley face a pleasant attitude. Better than others she had encountered before. She asked after employment in the caring profession if possible, but not hospital work. There was little to offer her except for home care and she had had enough of that in the past.

She came away subdued, and a bit downhearted and wondered if she had made a mistake in deciding to leave hospital life, a life she knew so well.

When she got home, Henry was so excited to see his mistress, he jumped up for the first kiss and cuddle and was his usual exuberant self, rushing back and forth. She had tried in vain to stop him from jumping up, never managing to curtail that activity. Moyra started to prepare food for the evening. Then they both sat on the settee close to the fire she had lit earlier. It sent out a lovely warmth and made the room cosy. She went over to turn the television on; there was a hard bang on the front door.

She didn't have many callers to the house, that alone sent Henry barking and softly growling.

"Hush, boy, stop it now!" She was afraid of who might be there at this time of night. Mind you it was only seven in the evening.

The knock came again, and a voice called out. "It's only me from two doors down. Nothing to worry about."

She cautiously opened the door just a crack. There stood her neighbour whom she met earlier in the week when taking Henry out for his walk.

"Hello, I know we have only just met, but do you mind if I come in? I wanted to talk to you about something. My name is Terry," he said as he held out his hand toward hers.

Surprised, Moyra was silent but at the same time, ushered him in. "Please come into the lounge; there's a fire on and it's much warmer in there."

"Thanks a bunch. And, your name is?"

"I'm Moyra."

"How do you do, pet." He said in a northern country accent. Perhaps it was Derbyshire; she couldn't be sure but she'd worked with a lass who was from that part of the country.

"What is it you wish to discuss, please sit down." She didn't ask him to take his coat off as she didn't want him to be too comfortable when they had only just met. It struck Moyra that her dealings with men except for male nurses, doctors, and patients on a professional level were about her limit.

"You know you told me this morning that you're looking for work, well I have something in mind I thought may interest you. That is, of course, if you haven't got something else in the pipeline."

She was so taken aback that she said, "Well, I've been looking for some time and not to date found anything suitable."

"Ah-ha, maybe you could be in luck then."

"What do you mean?" she said, startled at this revelation.

"I own a men and women's luxury end clothing shop and need a manager and I thought you might make the perfect employee for the job. What do you think, lass?"

"This is all a bit sudden, Mr...? ...Oh, sorry, I don't know your last name."

"It's Jones, but do please call me Terry. You'd like it there you know, it's a clean job, not like the one you're used to where you have to clean up people's excrement and other ghastly such-likes."

"What would you know about the nursing profession, if you've only known men's and women's clothing all your working life? It's work that takes a special person to do, you know. Someone who cares about their fellow human beings," she said defensively.

"Well, if you feel that way, why are you about to leave it?"

"That's none of your business, and I have things to do, so I would like you to leave now; if you don't mind."

"Well, I do mind, but I can see you want to be on your own. Bye, for now, I hope we can talk again."

And with that, she ushered Mr. Terry Jones straight to the front door he came in through and without another word, she shut the door behind him, turned around and leaned up against it sighing.

She thought long and hard about what he'd said to her. How dare he consider her work to be so demeaning.

She walked back to the kitchen and made herself a cup of coffee. Her loving dog came alongside and together, they went and sat on the couch. Moyra stroked Henry's head as she told him. "How dare he, he doesn't know that I want to be able to spend more time with you. And, I shall not be the one to tell him so."

Mr. Jones became one of the first many gentleman friends who came into and left her life almost as quickly as they came into it.

One or two appeared as though they lived on the edge of trouble.

The occasional one who smelled of the *essence de pub* and a couple who suffered self-righteous loathing.

When, oh, when, she thought to herself, *will I find someone who I shall be in simpatico with?*

Chapter Six

B y now, she had left her nursing career behind and found a comfortable niche in the adjacent town as a secretary to a kindly solicitor who cared about those who sought his expertise. He would often chat with her toward the end of the day, sharing the miseries of some people's lives and beaming joyously when considering the possibilities of a better future for other's troubles and dilemmas.

Rarely did he ever mention Moyra's personal circumstances; however, this evening he ventured as to what they might be. He asked her if she was happy in her life and what, if anything, she would care to change?

"Well, Mr. Hargreaves, I think I should like to find someone to share my life with. I've yet to meet the right one."

"A nice-looking lady like you, I would have thought you had them constantly knocking at your door."

"Sadly, no. But I shan't give up hope just yet."

"I should think not. You are sure to find happiness in the strangest of places as it happened to Mrs. Hargreaves and me. We met as mature folks, married and we have lived happily ever after. I know it sounds unusual and perhaps a bit corny these days. We were blessed with a daughter who died at the age of twelve from a form of Leukaemia. We were heartbroken when we lost Sophie, thank the Lord we had each other."

"I am so sorry to hear that, Sir," Moyra said stepping toward her boss and touching his arm. "I had no idea. I just surmised you had no family as you have never spoken of any children."

"Oh, it was a long time ago, but we still talk of her from time to time. The initial grieving was all-consuming, but that changes as does everything in this life of ours. Nothing stays the same forever, you know. Now I must be getting home, or I shall be in trouble as supper will be waiting.

As he left that evening and went out into the cold, winter night air, she watched him go down the steps and take out a hanker-chief and she thought she saw him wipe away a tear, then blow his nose.

The dynamics changed between them after that night. He was always trying to help her find a suitable partner, and she endeavoured to stifle the inner gift of empathy granted to most who work or have worked in the caring profession for fear of his misinterpretation.

41

She began to believe finding a suitable partner, in fact, perhaps even the love of her life would never make an appearance that was until the day on a walk with Henry. She saw an older man in the distance running after his dog who'd decided to chase another one on the loose and the other side of the field. As she walked closer, she saw he was getting anxious about this dog on the loose.

"I have only just let her off and look at where she's got to. Oh, troubles brewing; I just know it."

"I'll help you to catch her if you wish."

"Yes, thanks, that would be great."

And so, a romance began.

Michael was older than Moyra, by some seventeen years. However, she had an insatiable need to be near him and in the early days, they could not keep their hands off each other. They married and settled down in a cosy bungalow because he told her they needed to consider the future and how he may not be able to manage stairs.

She went along with it for the sake of harmony as after the first flourish of love and lust; she realised the man had quite a nasty temper. It bothered her at first and she spoke to him about it and that he needed to temper that sort of behaviour. He vowed he would, that he was sorry, and that he would ensure it didn't happen again.

She wondered if his lack of control may well have been the reason his first marriage failed. That was years ago, though, and she considered that by now, the years would have mellowed him and self-control would have taken over. He had long retired and after the early years, she wanted to get a job working with animals. She had always loved them and after her beloved Henry crossed the rainbow bridge, she had not had another dog. Her husband had not even wanted another dog. This made her unhappy, and she begged until her resolve eventually failed as she realised it was a pointless exercise.

All she now wished for was that she was again on her own.

Chapter Seven

A few years later they moved to the South East of England. Moyra had sold the family home in Chesterfield for a pittance and made sure that her siblings received their share from the sale. She told her goodbyes to the neighbours and friends and left the only place she had known for all her life.

She was nervous about leaving and being with a man with whom she now knew she had little in common with and in whom she had lost interest.

They moved to Surrey, a county in the South of England, not far from London, and she managed to get work on a local farm which enabled her to be close to the animals she loved so much. Not just dogs, Moyra loved all animals. The work was hard especially in winter when mud and muck were the very definitions of repulsive. She considered that challenges are what make life interesting, and she firmly believed that overcoming them is what makes life meaningful. She endured all this for two reasons. First, she could get away from the depression of home life; and second, she wallowed in her love of the animals she tended.

The day came when she met by chance a total stranger, Tom Ursuline, a famous American actor, who surprised her when he called to her to help with directions.

He promised that she would be hearing from him after he returned to the States.

And she did, it was a crisp, bright, winter day when the sun shone, and the world looked beautiful with its silver glint shimmering across the paths and garden. As she looked through their frosted glass window, she noticed a delivery van pull up. Her stomach did a flip as she saw it stop outside their gate. Her husband, by now a very old man, was asleep in his favourite dark brown leather armchair long passed its sell-by date.

The doorbell rang, and she looked in the mirror as she passed to check on the way she looked, tucked the hair over her ear lobes, then opened the door. A huge bouquet was handed to a Moyra French. Her smile lasted for some minutes as she read the small card accompanying them. Yes, he had kept his promise and sent the flowers to her to say thanks. The card read, "To Moyra, the lovely lady who kindly showed me the way that day. From an admirer."

Yes, it must be from him, and of course, he couldn't put his real name on the card. That would never do. He couldn't have members of the public knowing his real name for fear they would go to the press in the hope of financial reward.

How would she explain the flowers and card to her husband as she had chosen not to tell him about the chance meeting two weeks before? Perhaps she'd say they were from a friend she worked with and a week earlier of her upcoming birthday. Yes, that would be the right thing to do. The accompanying card would be tucked away in her secret stash of money and odds and ends she devotedly treasured.

She took them into where he sat sleeping, touched his arm, and asked if he would like a cup of tea.

"Look what the local florist just delivered. Did you not hear the bell?"

"No, must have been asleep."

"Who the devil sent you those, I take it they are for you?"

"Yes, they are for me from a girl at work she thought my birthday was today. Obviously, she got it wrong."

"Lucky you. That reminds me, when is your birthday, anyway? S'pose I ought to make some sort of effort."

"Yes, that would make a change."

"Don't you bloody well start on me, madam. I'm not in the mood."

With that, Moyra left the sitting room, went to the kitchen and made tea for them both. She put the flowers into the only vase she possessed. They looked lovely. She wanted to keep them going as long as she could. So, she took them to the coldest place in the bungalow which happened to be the little private place she considered her haven. There was no central heating as he refused to have gas connected when the opportunity arose. He said they didn't need it and that the winters were not that cold to warrant the cost of running it each year. So, there was no warmth in her home in more ways than one. She needed to add several layers of clothing in the winter or she would have frozen. He told her that it was far healthier to add layers than have central heating, anyway. Still, she went there often to read and ponder what had become of her; a life she deeply regretted entering. She was lonely and in need of some changes in her life.

The first thing she thought about doing was to get in touch with her admirer and thank him for the beautiful flowers. They had stayed fresh and only started to show signs of their end after three weeks. She tended them every day, making sure there was enough water and added some plant feed top up each week. When they were finished, she earnestly set about finding Tom.

She had a nearly new computer she bought from a second-hand store in the town nearby. Sadly, she was in no way computer literate. Moyra delved into *Twitter* and *Facebook* and found out that she could find friends on her phone on *WhatsAp*. She spent as long as she could get away with on these sites, trying desperately hard alone to learn the ins and outs, pitfalls and possible scams. Although not altogether computer literate, she had worked in an office and computers were her daily tool for secretarial work.

After a month, she considered herself confident enough to have a go at finding some friends online. She had a feeling that Tom would be out there somewhere. She had heard recently he had joined several on-line sites and was determined to find him. She connected to *Whatsap*, *Facebook,* and *Twitte*r. After so long thinking she was on the right track to find him, she turned her attention to one of the daily papers reporting that he had indeed signed up to Instagram. Now she knew she had the right Tom Ursuline. However, she had noticed how many Toms seemed to out there and how on earth was one supposed to know who the real one was. Having already signed up for *Facebook* and *Twitter,* she had found Tom there. How happy she was knowing that this gorgeous man whom she had long admired and who seemed to take an interest in her was now on her radar, after all, he had sent her such a beautiful, huge, expensive-looking, bouquet, with the message, "To the lovely lady who kindly showed me the way."

Her search now over; she contemplated long and hard about how she would word her first message to Tom on *Instagram* messaging. She pondered the content in her head for days before she plucked up the courage to write it. She did not want to appear to be too formal; neither did she wish to alarm the celebrity with a chat of her feelings for him. So, it should be short, sweet, and to the point. She had read some comments others had written, all sweet and sugary with kisses and hearts and the like after divulging their love for him. One even called herself the future Mrs. Ursuline.

Her newfound confidence and being left on her own for long periods these days as a result of her husband's sleep complexities gave her the time to explore all the internet offered. As she sat in her, what she now referred to as her office, she looked out of the window facing the front garden and saw two squirrels chasing one another along the garden fence. She always found that scene so fascinating. Then as if by magic, her friendly fox appeared. There he was in broad daylight. The animal didn't usually appear before twilight and he had not been coming much of late. She deduced the reason for that had to be he was finding a mate. It was the time of year for that to occur.

He was such a fine-looking creature, sporting some of his winter coat already, she thought that was early as it was only just the beginning of December. She left her seat and went to the back door. She knew he would go to that door from the front as that was where his food would be served. Moyra regularly travelled to a nearby farm to buy his food in the guise of dog bones and biscuits, along with a few tins of dog food slipped into the groceries furtively when she did the weekly shopping. She knew her hankering for another dog was the reason for all this activity; she also knew that it was a lost cause to hope any more.

Her marriage, what a mistake that was, crossed her mind on a pretty regular basis. What she didn't know was what on God's good earth was she going to do about it.

She had some angst as she thought back to her marriage vows and the man's age. How could she do such a thing as to leave him? Her upbringing had been somewhat religious, and she had always been told by her mother that marriage was for life and that you had to work at it. Even though that didn't sit well with the way, her mother's marriage had gone.

One day he saw her putting the shopping away and said, "What is that you're trying to hide. Is it what I think it is?"

An almighty row ensued as she tried to fight her corner, saying the poor creature was starving and needed feeding or would die.

"The best thing that could happen, they're vermin that kill the chickens and any other creature sick and ill or small enough to kill. You'd better not let me see the blighter or he'll feel the shot from my gun," he said with such vitriol she felt the tears sting her eyes.

From that day forward, she realised she must either stop feeding the fox or make sure he never saw the fox coming around.

The fox was a wild animal, and there was no way she'd be able to stop him coming around as the feeding had begun and they only left when it suited them, not the other way around.

She lived in fear and dread about what the outcome of this latest conversation could lead.

"Do you know something, Dave, I don't think you are very kind toward me or to animals and I would like to know the reason why."

"Don't be stupid woman; you don't know how lucky you are. Always trying to make yourself into a silk purse from a sows ear. You don't know how lucky you are that I took you in."

"Took me in, you bastard, how dare you! You married me because you said you loved me. And in the beginning, I was daft enough to think you meant it, but you've changed so much over the years."

From that day on, Moyra left the bedroom they shared and interestingly, she thought he didn't seem to be particularly bothered by it.

Chapter Eight

After much hesitation and anxiety, she began to compose her first message to Tom.

First Message

Dear Tom,

I received the beautiful flowers you sent me a week or two back. Sorry not to have been in touch with you before, but I had a job finding you on the social media. Thank you so much, so kind of you to think of me.

The flowers lasted for over three weeks and smelt wonderful filling the house with their perfume.

I love flowers and you must have guessed that my favourites were roses and chrysanthemums. I had no idea that one could obtain roses of such a variety of magnificent colours. I have never seen them here in England before.

You may not remember me but, just in case, I was the lady who told you how to get to the village you were heading to. Moyra French is my name.

I have been doing some research about your films and life. I hope you don't mind.

She finished by saying. I do hope to meet you again some day. Thanks again.

Before she had time to rewrite the last sentence, she inadvertently pressed the send button. She hadn't even signed the blasted text and then intensely worried as she knew she shouldn't have said how she would like to meet him again someday. She worried herself silly for a few days, not sleeping and avoiding her husband as much as possible.

On the fourth day, after the message was sent, she checked her Twitter account and was amazed to find she had a response from Tom Ursuline.

Reply

'Hello, thanks so much for the message. I was pleased you liked the flowers. Sorry not have got back to you before but I have been so busy filming the latest in the series.

How are things for you back in England. You should know that I found my destination with no worries at all. Hope to hear from you again soon.

Bye for now, lovely girl. Tom xxx. '

P.S. Of course I remember you.

She had no patience in waiting for an appropriate amount of time before messaging him again. So that night, when the house was still, and she was feeling wide awake, she opened her tablet and touched the *Twitter* messaging icon. *What should I say?* She kept mulling it over. He obviously liked her enough to reply to her thank you. There were not many celebrities who would even bother to do that. She considered. 'And he had called me lovely.'

After about an hour of writing the message, in her mind, she started to reply to Tom's message.

Message Two

> *Dear Tom,*
>
> *It was so good to hear from you recently. Thank you for thinking of me enough to write.*
> *I so enjoy chatting with my friends on here as in my real life I don't have so many friends. I am married but that is a bit of a misnomer. I don't wish to bother you with my problems but just to be able to talk to you sometimes is all I'm really asking. I hope you don't think I'm asking to much.'*
> *With all good wishes, Moyra.*

The days passed and there was no return message. She worried that she had said far too much, and he had been put off by it.

She spent several days moping around the house, checking her tablet at frequent intervals.

One day, as she was deeply ensconced in the technology, in came her husband, who looked as if he was living more on the edge of trouble than usual. "I'm going out!" he half-shouted.

"Oh, are you now and where do you intend to go at this time of night?"

"You can mind your own business, and don't wait up."

What on earth was going on? She could not help but stew.

She had noticed that lately, he was doing strange things such as the other evening, he went out in his pyjamas. He said he needed to check to see if the post had come because he was expecting some important papers.

When she asked, "What kind of papers?" he curtly replied to her and again told her to mind her own business.

"It's the middle of winter and dark outside. What on earth are you going out now for? The post comes early morning and you know that."

"I do, but I bet you haven't been down to check if we had any today."

"Yes, I did, and you saw me do it and come back and tell you that there was no post today."

"Go back inside, woman, and leave me alone," came the reply.

She did just that and settled down to one of her favourite programs on television.

He did no more than come back in empty-handed and strode over to the remote control, sat beside Moyra, and switched the program off. "It's time for bed now. It's too late to be up watching rubbish on the box."

Moyra was horrified at his behaviour and did no more than turn it back on yelling at him.

He stormed from the room.

"You silly old sod, you're losing your mind. You go to bed! It's not time for me."

Nothing more was said between them that day and for many days dwindling into the weeks after.

Chapter Nine

After a few weeks, another message came to her.

Reply

hello moyra

'Can I ask do you have whatsap on your phone if so we could talk there and that would be good or Hangouts. That way I will be able to send you photos and video's. Hope you don't mind me asking and sorry not to have been in touch for so long but my schedule is so busy now that we've started filming again. All you need to do is get a gmail account and let me have it. Here is my gmail address tursuline2442 Just send me yours when you get it. '

She could hardly contain herself, the girl almost wept with joy, as the man of her dreams wished to send her photos and videos of himself.

He wanted to send her more photos and videos not seen on *Instagram*. How wonderful was that? He kept on replying to her messages.

The smile she bore never left her face each time she received a message from Tom. Each one a little more caring and loving in his wording. They connected on *Instagram* and many photos and scenes were forthcoming from Tom's side.

Moyra got up later than usual one morning. She had breakfast later that day and meandered into the farm at about eleven in the morning.

"Well, well, what's this all about? I was beginning to get worried about you, you're never this late in. Has something happened?" Asked her boss.

"Oh, something has happened all right, sorry to be this late. I think I was in a dream since I got up this morning."

"If there is anything, I can do to help you, just let me know."

Jack Reams was a kindly sort of bloke, and she thoroughly enjoyed working for him. He was easy going and easy to get along with. His kindly nature stemmed from difficulties he'd shared with Moyra about his younger years. He had got into trouble with the law and his guilt led him to find the Lord and now he loved and cared for all surrounding his life.

He smoked his pipe almost constantly and harboured a chesty cough as a result.

She, being the hard worker, she was, found enjoyment being on the farm with him as they always got along well. That was the case right from the start of their working relationship. He never tried to convert her religious beliefs and seldom spoke of his.

The farm was large housing a variety of animals and two other handymen worked alongside Moyra and Jack Reams.

Her thoughts turned to Tom during the day. She wanted to respond to Tom immediately but changed her mind as the day wore on. Working alone, as she invariably did, made her get into the habit of talking to herself out loud. "I must not be stupid about this, but one day I may go over there to America, California, that's where I think he lives. Probably in some huge mansion of luxury living. He seems to like me, so I hope he does ask me over. I can make out that I'm going on holiday with a friend. God only knows who though, as I'm not that close to anyone."

As she mucked out the two horses stables later in the day, she was surprised to see the huge grey called Fritz come over and start nuzzling into her arm.

"What are you up to you, my beauty?" she whispered in his ear.

Fritz neighed the loudest neigh she had ever heard him utter. One of the hands, Peter, came in at that moment and said, "Wow, I've never heard him shout so loud. Must be a tryin' to tell you some in Moy's."

"You may be right; he is rather loud today."

She thought the great greys noisy interaction was some message, and it meant good things coming your way Moyra.

She needed to get on and make up for the lost time of the morning and worked as she smiled, even laughing out loud sometimes — something she had not done in many years.

After a day or two, she sent a message back to her new found friend. And what a friend she had found.

She thought about Tom constantly and conjured up a long and interesting message to send him when she returned home that evening. The days were getting longer as it was now spring. When she returned home that night, she had a major upheaval. As she entered the house, she felt something wasn't right. There were no lights on in the bungalow. As she entered the kitchen and turned on the light, she smelled something strange. Moyra tried hard to establish in her brain what it was, however, unsuccessfully.

Next, she wandered into her husband's side of the home, still in total darkness, and as she tried to open the door, she couldn't manage it as something heavy the other side impeded the movement.

She rushed to her nearest neighbour who was about a quarter of a mile away and banged hard on the door knocker. The man of the house came to the door. Moyra barely knew him, only having passed a few pleasantries as they passed each other when walking. They had never stopped to have a conversation.

"Hello, I'm so sorry to bother you, but I cannot get into the lounge at home and the place was in total darkness when I came in from work. Please can you come back with me as I don't have the strength to push the door open?"

Recognising her immediately, he duly obliged as he shouted back to somebody. "Just going to help the lass from up the road, she's got a bit of bother. Hope I won't be long."

He followed Moyra who started to dash back to her home. The neighbour shouted to her to come back and get in the car. "It will be quicker," he yelled.

Fortunately, he was a big man and strong as when they got back into the house; he managed alone to push the door open.

What greeted the pair was shocking. Moyra's husband was lying face down on the floor and the strange smell soon revealed that he had been trying to clean some tiles around the fireplace. It was covered in dirt and grime from the last winter's soot and likely many winter's before with ammonia spirit. The smell was overpowering.

"Oh, my God! Is he breathing?" she asked.

Her neighbour bent to where he lay and slowly turned him onto his back with great difficulty as his arm got stuck under his body in the movement. He was a bluish-red and the smell almost knocked him over.

"Quickly girl; call for an ambulance," he half-shouted to Moyra.

She did as she was told, and it took about ten minutes for the ambulance to arrive. During the waiting time, he remained still and did not appear to be breathing; however, her neighbour mentioned that he had seen some chest movement. He was so kind and stayed with her until the ambulance came and the two paramedics were phenomenal in their care for both

Moyra and the patient. They did every test within their power to do.

"He does not seem to be responsive, ma'am."

"Call me, Moyra, please."

"Does he have any underlying conditions?"

"Yes, he has a weak heart and is on tablets. Can't remember what they're called. I'll go and get them. He is also losing his mind a bit. He is seventy-seven years old. She was concerned as she had taken so little interest in her husband's health of late and didn't have the latest low-down on what exactly was the matter with him.

"Well, Moyra, his pulse is weak and thready; and his E.C.G is not particularly good. But he is not dead, and that means we may be lucky."

Luck, she thought. *Why is that lucky? The bastard has been such a sod to me over the past years I really don't care.*

Then, she found herself consumed with guilt almost in the same thinking process.

The paramedics fetched a stretcher and gently lifted Arthur onto it. They suggested to Moyra that she would need to follow the ambulance by car as they would be unable to bring her back home. Also, she was told that the house needed to be fully aired before she could return to stay there.

She duly followed the ambulance in her car. Upon arriving, she had trouble finding out which room they took him. She thought it would be likely to be the Accident and Emergency Department, but when she got there, he was not. She was told by a large woman in a blue uniform, who looked mostly annoyed that she had been disturbed from the action she was on, that he might have been taken straight to the cardiac centre.

That was a considerable walk away from the main building and sat a good half-mile from where she currently found herself.

She was quite exhausted when she finally reached her destination and was directed to a small room where someone would soon come and find her to provide information about her husband.

As she waited, she pulled out her I phone and dialled his family. His elderly sister was thriving and living in a warden-controlled accommodation.

"Hello, is Jane there?"

"Speaking."

"Oh, Jane; it's Moyra, Arthur's wife. Could you please pass a message onto his sister and tell her he has been admitted to hospital? I don't know what is wrong at the moment. I'm waiting to hear. I found him unconscious when I got home from work. There was the most awful smell of ammonia in the room. We know that because the empty bottle must have spilled over when he fell."

"Yes, of course, I will Moyra. And I'm so sorry to hear about this."

"Yes, it will be a shock for her, but I think she has the right to know. I think he's very sick."

"Please tell her that I will call back when we have some more news. Thanks, Jane."

His sister, although old, was sharp as a razor. Having all her wits about her, although a blessing in some ways in others, it wasn't, and the old girl had tried exceedingly hard to be allowed to move in with her brother and Moyra. Moyra had the common sense to avoid this situation. Objecting, she told him that if that were to happen, she would be leaving. Moyra felt that his sister didn't think much of her, making that clear when they were together with snide, hurtful remarks in her direction.

With that done, she stood by the drink machine as time seemed to be at a standstill. She stared at the floor, thinking. *What the heck shall I do now? My marriage isn't good, but I don't relish being on my own either. He looks so sick and the staff in the Cardiac Department told me things did not look good.*

"Stop self-pitying," she scolded herself, and with that took off to the area where her husband was warded. When she managed to find the nurse in charge, she asked if she could see him and if a diagnosis had been made.

"The doctors are coming up soon and we should have some news for you then. Did he have any underlying condition before this happened?"

"Yes, he was diagnosed with heart disease quite a while back. I don't remember exactly when, but it's been several years."

"Don't worry; we can find out more from the G.P."

Just then, the doctors all arrived as an entourage of eminent looking people, both men and women.

Moyra thought she had never seen so many women becoming doctors before. They were certainly not around when she was a child in the Sanatorium.

They went to the first patient while Moyra stood at the end of her husband's bed. Then they came to where she stood and the one who looked like the most senior and with a pompous manner said, "And who do we have here?"

Showing fear and uncertainty, Moyra answered, "I am this man's wife," pointing toward where her husband lay.

"Right," said the pompous one, "we had better take a look and see what we can find, hadn't we?"

A bit shocked by this nonchalant attitude around an unconscious man made her feel even more uneasy. They let her stay with them behind the curtains. The boss ordered blood and radiology tests.

"This may help to find out what the problem is. I suggest you go and get a coffee or something. Take your mind off things a bit, dear. And whatever is that ghastly smell around our man?"

"That, we think is where he was trying to do some glass cleaning, and when he fell, the bottle of ammonia spilled."

Bloody cheek, what a horrible man, Moyra thought. She decided to take heed and went to find the canteen and coffee.

It was the first drink she had taken in about six hours, and she hadn't realised just how thirsty she was. She stayed there a while and then decided to take a walk in the gardens. It was early June, and summer was trying to push through the cold and wet weather they seemed to have been experiencing for such a long time. She pulled her coat up around her neck as she wandered along a stone slab path and found a seat.

The seat was in memory of "Doris a dearly loved wife, mother and grandmother" who had died the previous year.

She stayed there for about an hour and then began to shiver as daylight nudged the night aside. As the birds started their morning chorus, she decided it was time to return to the ward.

The blood test results hadn't arrived. However, the X-rays revealed a hugely enlarged heart.

When the blood tests eventually arrived, it was evident that her husband was not going to survive this episode, and she was told to prepare herself for the worse.

"Do you wish to stay at the hospital?" said one of the pretty, young nurses in a kindly manner.

She replied that she did and that she would stay by her husband's bedside.

He was never to regain consciousness and died that morning.

Moyra felt so strange and could not understand why she did not cry. She just felt numb and had no idea what was being said to her as she left the ward. Everything seemed hazy and the sounds of the person's voice talking to her kept disappearing. She thought she'd be unable to drive home safely.

She got into her car and thought and the only thought coming and going was, *Hooray, now I can get a dog.* How could she be thinking this way when her husband had only just left this world? But there it was, she did.

Chapter Ten

She informed all those whom she felt she needed too, letting them know when the funeral was to be and where.

The neighbour who helped her the night of her dead husband's collapse came to see how she was doing.

"You have probably heard the news that Arthur died in the morning after the night he was taken in. Thank you so much for helping me. I was frightened and if it hadn't been for you coming to the rescue, I don't know how I'd have coped." She handed him a bottle of whiskey squirrelled from her late husband's drink cabinet. "I don't know much about drink as I'm not too keen on the stuff, but I do recall Arthur saying this was a good one. I was meaning to bring it round to you, but I have been so busy telling people and getting everything sorted out. I'm sorry not to have told you in person."

"Don't worry about that, Moyra, we had already heard, you know what it's like around here and how news travels like wildfire. Now come over later and have supper with us. June said to ask you to join us."

"Thank you, Stanley, that's most kind. I will take you up on that offer, what time shall I come? The funeral is to be next Thursday at three p.m. and at the Brookwood cemetery. You know the one that everyone in these parts seems to use. It will be a Humanist ceremony as he did not believe in God or the church. The undertakers have been very good in helping me through all the necessary paperwork and what I had to do, you know all the legal stuff that needs to be organised. I wouldn't have known where to begin. The lady conducting the service has been so kind and helpful too."

After he left, she got to thinking about what Stanley had said about news travelling fast. Wouldn't these neighbours be surprised to know that she was in contact with Tom Ursuline? *Now wouldn't they?*

Moyra went the few doors down from where she lived and had a relatively pleasant evening with the kind folks who did sincerely appear to care. The house was so welcoming and cosy, not like anything she had known in her own home for years. They talked about when she hoped to return to work and what her future plans might consist of. It was getting late, and she decided to say, "Well, thanks so much, I have enjoyed this evening. When I have the house in some semblance of an order, I will return the favour."

As she left the house, her thoughts turned to her next message to Tom. She wondered how long it might be before he or even she suggested they meet up. She was keen to do that as soon as possible and fancied a trip to California. She'd never been to the States and took it upon herself to get hold of every bit of literature and as much information from the internet about the place she could.

The funeral was held on one of the worst days you could imagine in June. It rained from morning to night. Everything on the and in the ground was bone dry as there had been a long spell without rain. So, the gardeners were delighted. However, attending your husband's funeral on such a day left a deep, damp feeling throughout the entire congregation which of course, one would expect, although intensified by the weather.

The few attendees came back on the invitation of Moyra to her small home; they wandered in, attempting to avoid the inclement weather. That was impossible; so, on arrival, all were wet, cold, hungry, and thirsty. Moyra had not given much thought or effort in her accommodating the funeral attendees lost in thought, as she was these days.

There were a few sandwiches hurriedly made that the morning, a couple of bottles of wine, one red and one white which was soon gone and all that remained was tea, coffee, lemonade or squash.

She chatted with her siblings and found out all the latest happenings in their lives that she considered being far more boring than her own was going to be. She was also anxious for them to leave so that she could get down to her communications with her friend.

"What are you going to do in the future?" Jane said, anxiously.

"I shall remain here. Why would I want to leave, and I now have a job I love and enjoy going to work each day? So, nothing to leave for."

"I was just thinking that you may wish to be closer to some of your family that's all. But you're ever independent and capable. Are you not, Moyra?" her sister complained.

"Yes, and a good job. Think about how it would have been if I'd not been there to take care of mother and help raise you. Anyway, I've got plans. I intend to have the holiday of a lifetime and probably go to America. California in fact, I have always wanted to go there and now there is nothing to stop me."

The conversations carried on a little while longer, and then as though a major accident occurred the funeral attendees were out the door, and on their way back to their own lives and familiarity.

After the initial shock of it all, she somehow summoned the courage to consider the situation not to be all that bad. After all was said and done, they had been estranged for a considerable length of time and now she was free.

However, she found certain aspects of this major life-changing event and being alone difficult to adjust to. She sorted all the financial matters with the bank manager thus ensuring the regular bills were paid. It was then she realised her husband's pension was smaller than she thought and her wages meagre. She would have to manage money exceptionally carefully. She thought her husband had some savings;

unfortunately, this was not the case and not having any family nearby for support added to the difficulties.

Tom and California now became her life's primary focus. That was along with her desire to buy a dog. Would it be a puppy, or would it be a rescue dog? That seemed to be the novel way of getting a pet these days and she hoped her long, long-held dream would one day soon come true. She had so much to think about.

***

Message Three

My dear Tom, I am so sorry for not being in touch with you before now, but my life has been to put it mildly extreme.

My husband just died, he was old and had severe heart problems, so in a way it was expected. But quite a shock as it was so sudden.

How have you been? Are you working and what are you working on? I can't wait for your next film to be released and I shall be there in London for the opening night to see you again on the red carpet, that will just be wonderful.

Reply

My dear Moyra, I am so sorry to hear the sad news of your husbands death. This must have been the worst kind of shock.

I had been wondering how you were as I had not heard from you for a while.

I hope you are getting above it lately.

Perhaps you should have a holiday soon. Bye for now Tom xx

Message Four

Yes, a holiday would be a blessed relief, providing I can get time away from my work. I so want to know more about your life Tom. What films are you making these days? Are you as busy as you ever have been? Do you have time to even have a date with someone? All these things I would love to hear about.

My life is pretty dull It's all work and then sorting out everything to do with the will and his family and everyone telling me what I should and shouldn't do. And all I really want to do is to be having conversation with you.Please reply soon, even sooner if possible.

I so love to hear from you M xxx

Three weeks passed.

Reply

sorry to have left it a while as you can rightly guess its due to the work schedule. I'm a bit down right now as things have not been as I want them.life is a drudge now and I have had problems at work and argued with producers. I would have done stuff different but he don't agree.What's the weather like over there?

Have to go now,

Bye.Tom x

Message Five

Oh, my dear man, this is not good news. I have read that you too do some producing and directing. If I understand it correctly, the producer pays for the work and the director does just that and directs the actors.

72

Correct me if I'm wrong.

You don't have to be worried, things do have a way of working out and you can always talk to me. You must remember the old saying 'a trouble shared is a trouble halved.'

Speak again soon, Moyra x

Reply

Hello I'm very busy my end and I don't get much time to myself these days. Its my fault I know that and that its because I'm a workaholic and all that stuff and I never have time to do the stuff I really want and need to do. And what's the weather doing over there. Also the public is making many demands on my time.

Tom.

Message Six

Oh Tom; it's so good to hear from you. The weather is fine at the moment. But the weather in Britain, as you likely well know, is unpredictable at best. I take it all is well. I do appreciate how busy you are, and I understand.

You don't tell me much about your films or what you're working on. And as for a holiday I think that is a fantastic idea.

How would you feel if I came over to California and stayed in a hotel and then we perhaps could meet up?

Bye now,
Mx

Chapter Eleven

There was a considerable distance between this message and Tom's reply. Moyra was beginning to think it was all too much too soon on her part and she sat at home staring into empty spaces night after night. Then going to her tablet and looking always looking to see if a reply had come in, she got to a point where she felt she would need to write again, just in case he had not received the previous message. Then common sense prevailed, and she considered why would a famous superstar be interested in a country bumpkin like her. He could have his pick of the most beautiful women in the world and from what she read about him had done just that in the past. Then, on the other hand, she considered that maybe, just maybe, he fancied an ordinary girlfriend who had no links what-so-ever with the world of acting and fame and one who no longer had ties and was now a free agent.

When she decided to turn in that night, she went over to the mirror in her bedroom and looked directly at her body. She brushed her long grey-streaked, dyed, dark blond hair and just stared at herself, eventually deciding that she looked pretty good for her age, considering all she had been through recently. Her skin was in good condition and her hair lustrous. She only had a few lines on her slightly weathered face, unusual for a person working outside as she did in all weathers and seasons and no bags had yet developed under her eyes.

So why should he not like her and want to be her friend that may even develop into something more than friendship or was she daydreaming and being unrealistic?

All these thoughts and intense feelings kept mulling over keeping her awake most of the night, so much so that she turned the alarm clock off, turned over and went back to sleep. Feeling embarrassed when she finally awoke, she rang her workplace and said how sorry she was but she had been feeling unwell and with the terrible headache, she now suffered she would not be going into work. Later that day Moyra found herself ready to write another message to her dear friend.

Message Seven

Hello Tom, its Moyra. You seemed to be a bit down in your recent contacts. Are you all right? I hope your not going down with anything nasty. I suppose you're around people all the time. And people always have nasties like colds and flu and all of that sort of thing. You would be telling me wouldn't you if you were to be ill.

I need to tell you something, I think about you most of the time now. At work, at home, out shopping or doing the housework. You're always on my mind Tom. I just needed to tell you this.

With my love M.XXX

Reply

hi,we have to be careful I cannot afford any bad or adverse publicity right now. I'm doing quite a lot of work with my parents and aunt and uncle and my time is very low.

Don't be desperate we may be able to meet.however I am.I am in desperate need of free cash as at the moment all my funds are heavily tied up. Would there be a chance that you might be able to send a bit to me? My mind is made up that I have to help my families needs before my own.

I don't know what you believe or if you are Christian or not. Maybe you don't even believe in God !!! But I do and I need money. Would you be willing to send some over

Message Eight

Oh, my dear man. I am sorry to hear you are going through difficulties. I suppose that's part of life's rich pageant. Yes, I do go to church on the odd occasion. I'm not a regular and to be honest I have a few doubts about religion. When I was younger and nursing, many of us had grave doubts that a God even existed and I think that was all about if he was all omnipotence then why would he allow suffering, especially with the little ones.

Having said all that, how much are you in need of?

I have a little savings but not that much.
Let me know in your next message.
With love Mx

The reply to her last message came rather more speedily than those received each time before. Moyra was, of course, over the moon about this and could not contain herself from opening and reading it directly when it arrived.

Reply

oh my dear friend, dear friend that is so good of you, Of course, you know I will repay you. You will not be out of pocket.

It's $3000 are you going to send it? You can come over if you like and bring it with you.

Perhaps we shall be able to get it together when you're over.

Don't worry if you ain't got it though. I think I'll understand.

My family are in great need right now and are on to me about it always.

Hope you O.K.and I look forward to meeting up with you.

TomXXX

Message Nine

I think it's a good idea for me to come over with it for you. I have not had a holiday for years now. I really could do with one, and of course, getting to meet and know you better, now that would be the top brick off the

chimney for me. I shall make all the arrangements and let you know the date and my time of arrival.
With much love and I cannot wait to see you again.
Love Moyra xxx

That night Moyra stood in front of her long mirror in the bathroom and examined her body in a way not done before. She had been fortunate to keep a reasonable girlie figure of which she was proud. She put it down to all the heavy lifting and heaving she had to do on the farm.

However, she recognised that a degree of detail was needed to smarten herself up before she could ever think of meeting up with her friend.

First things first, she decided to make a hair appointment, and this was somewhat of a revolution. She walked out of that salon with her head held high, looking like a million dollars. She had her hair once again cut and styled into a bob. It was a grand new style, and the stylist said, "It's taken years off of you, love. You must always wear it this way. You've got beautifully thick hair that would be the envy of so many of my customers."

Next came a visit to the dentist. It had been a while since she had a check-up and she knew her teeth needed a good clean and maybe she would even consider whitening them. She'd read that in the States many people now had this treatment carried out.

She was sorely disappointed when Dr. Phelps, her dentist of many years said, "Quite a while since you last came; now, is it not Mrs. French? And of course, that in itself had taken its toll on your mouth and oral hygiene."

She needed four fillings, and a considerable amount of cleaning before her mouth would be in decent shape, once again.

"You've always had beautiful teeth and regular check-ups. What on earth happened?"

"My husband died a few months ago, quite unexpectedly, and life has been so busy with all that goes with the aftermath."

"I am sorry to hear about your husband, Moyra, do you mind if I call you by your first name?" Her dentist enquired.

"When would you like to make an appointment? I suggest you do not leave it too long before you come back. See if my receptionist can fit you in next week. Would that fit in with your plans?"

"I don't appear to have much choice in the matter, now do I? What do you think about whitening? I was considering having some of that as I thought my teeth were looking a bit yellowish?"

"I am the wrong person to be asking that as I neither do it nor believe in it. I don't think it enhances your appearance. If that's the reason you wish to have it done, your teeth are a perfect colour as they are."

At that juncture, she chose to leave and on her way out of the surgery, asked if an appointment could be made for her the following week.

She checked in her handbag for the diary she always carried, which this day she'd forgotten to bring.

The summer was well established now, and the trees were in full leaf, and flowers bloomed in abundance. One of her favourites, Jasmine, traversed her nostrils with its delicious scent as she walked away from the surgery toward her car.

When she reached the car park, she had a job recalling where she'd left it and panic began to set in. She walked the whole of the car park and her car was nowhere to be seen. She called the police, and they told her she needed to come into the station as she would need to give all the details of what now appeared to be a stolen vehicle.

Grudgingly agreed. The police station was over on the other side of town and she had to wait for ages for the right bus to come along to take her. On arrival, she was sent to an empty room with a desk and two chairs and there she waited pushing her bag back and forth along the desk until a uniformed policewoman came in. The questioning began and Moyra couldn't help but think she was being treated like a criminal. All the forthcoming questions mortified her she was expected to answer.

"Madam, you are sure you locked the vehicle, aren't you?"

"Yes, of course, I did. I'm not that stupid. I know what it's like in this town."

Then a deluge of questions was fired at her one after the other. When the time came for Moyra to leave the station, she felt positively insuperable. One of the police were going to give her a lift back home, for which she was eternally grateful. No buses went anywhere near to where she lived.

Her driver was a youngish man who spoke to her in a flirty kind of way, and she too responded to the attention she was being given. She didn't know what was happening to her as all her feelings since her connection with Tom were somewhat exaggerated. Moyra seemed to be in a brighter place these days.

She thanked the driver for the lift and offered to give him money for a drink. He refused and said that such was frowned upon and could even end up with dismissal from the force had he accepted.

She spent an age trying to find out where her car might have been left and why the police did not act more quickly than they were doing. Eventually, the vehicle was found abandoned and a wreck. When she went to collect it from the garage, where the police had it taken to, the look was one of horror because the car was unrecognisable. She felt the tears stinging her eyes as the chap at the garage handed her the keys and said, "It's still drivable miss."

Drivable, and what's it going to cost me to have the item put back to normal, she thought.

They talked, and she realised that it was only a heap of junk and that maybe she should treat herself to a new one.

And that is precisely what she did. The garage was delighted to be able to sell her a car, rather than having to try to make a sack of rubbish into perfection, which would have been the case had they attempted to repair it.

That night she got into a serious texting conversation with Tom

Message Ten

Oh Tom, my car was stolen and when the police found it, it was a drivable wreck. I could have had it

repaired but the insurance was sufficient for me to be able to afford a new car. I had to put a bit towards it but not that much. I have bought a bright blue, Ford Focus and it's my pride and joy. Its a wonderful car and quite economical. I shall be arriving at 12:00 noon on the 30th August. I hope you will send someone to meet me. Can you let me know? If not, I shall make my way to The Hilton Hotel that's where I hope to stay, I haven't booked it yet.

Can't wait to see you.

Love Moyra xxx

Chapter Twelve

The flight was booked. Even the taxi to take Moyra to Heathrow Airport had been ordered. It would be a twelve-hour flight, which she was not looking forward to taking. She did not like flying and had limited experience of it always preferring to stay in the United Kingdom for holidays rather than having to fly anywhere. The plane would arrive at LAX International airport in Los Angeles.

The evening before she took off for the holiday, with her few clothes newly purchased for the occasion and the money for Tom safely protected in her luggage, she thought about how much money it had amounted to with the trip, her new car, clothes and the money she was about to transport to her friend.

You could not count the number of times the clothes she chose to wear to travel went out of the wardrobe then back in, and then a new set tried on and discarded. In the finish, she stuck to the items she'd initially chosen. She looked for any last-minute messages and indeed there was one from Tom.

Reply

> hi,moyra,as you know I shall not be able to meet you at the airport because of the publicity. And I always have body guards alongside. Just in case.You know what I mean, don't you.
> So I will send Grant to pick you up and he will take you to de hotel. His a close friend and honest guy, you like him.
> See you soon.
>
> Tom xx

She fully understood the situation and went to bed earlier than usual and of course, failed to get any sleep at all. The taxi arrived early and off she went glad that she did not have to leave any pets behind that she had seriously thought about acquiring.

The airport was a maze of people, the hustle and bustle everywhere. It had been such a long time since she had flown anywhere, she had forgotten what overcrowded and dystopian these places could be and she loathed crowds at the best of times. This was a means to an end, and she had to put up with it. The flight proved to be an enormous hurdle to overcome. She was squeezed between a huge bloke of about twenty stones on one side; a faint whiff of body odour drifting from his direction to hers, and a miserable, grizzler, with a mother on the other. However, there was little turbulence on the twelve-hour non-stop flight. The plane appeared to be full, so she didn't even bother to ask to move seats. About halfway through the flight, she managed to get a little sleep, more through exhaustion than anything else. The peace and quiet were such a relief after the child fell asleep on his mother's lap.

The fat one started snoring loudly, and that woke her up with such a startle, she wondered where she was for a moment or two.

Reality soon hit home, and she asked the fat one to move a little so she could stretch her legs and visit the facilities.

Then it came time to eat. The food looked less than appetising; however, she was hungry, so she decided to go for it. By now, the excitement of the whole adventure was starting to set in. She felt a permanent smile develop, and the powerful feeling of all being well with the world overcame her and the smile remained on her face for the rest of the journey.

The plane arrived a little ahead of schedule, and Moyra hoped this would not upset any of the meeting plans. She tried to look past the mother and child to see out of the window, but this was virtually impossible. As she moved across, the child awoke and started to create havoc. The mother was becoming frantic trying to calm the child and eventually asked for the hostess' help in placating him. Clearly used to dealing with such crisis, the air steward took the little one from the mother and walked him up and down the aisle with the bribery of sweets being found at the end of their trail. This for a little child being the pot of gold at the end of the rainbow. He was suitably silent until the plane started to descend. His snotty nose depicted the possibility of an ear problem and his screaming began proving this to be the case.

He was distraught, in great pain and even the constant feeding of sweets did nothing to settle him. The descent kept going for over thirty minutes and we finally touched down at LAX airport.

This next part of her adventure was nothing but fraught with trial and tribulation. Customs were officious and never smiled making her feel as though she was a hardened criminal trying to escape from the land where the crime took place.

This was supposed to be the land of milk and honey, friendship, love, and the land of the free, but she felt it to be anything but that. Next, she was told, "Come with me" by a mountain of a woman towering at least a foot above her.

"Why do you want me to come with you?" Moyra asked pitifully.

As such, the woman seemed to think Moyra may have something to hide. Well to some extent, that was true. She was coming over to meet up with her friend and international superstar Tom Ursuline.

She was marched into a side room and asked to stand straight. The woman began running her hands up and down Moyra's sides, across her chest, and then the inside of her legs. She thought for a moment that there was to be an internal, and she was alone with this one woman and no chaperone making her feel extremely uncomfortable.

It soon became apparent that she had no contraband, cigarettes, or alcohol on her person. So, the hand luggage was first for the third degree and then everything was discharged from her suitcase.

"What is this all in aid of?" Moyra protested.

"Nothing to worry about, dear. We do this from time to time on people coming in from the U.K. It seems you are hiding nothing so off you go and have a nice day ma'am," she said in such a condescending way that Moyra felt like slapping her in the mouth. She resisted this overwhelming desire.

She left her holding pen and walked toward the exit and was amazed to see the throng of people waiting for friends, relatives and Heaven alone knows who, some standing with placards and the person expected names clearly written. A lady walking along next to her said, "This is nothing; if we had been out sooner, it would have been a battlefield. Some advantage of being searched, don't you think?"

There stood a tall, good looking man wearing a Stetson hat and holding a plaque with her name written. She smiled and sort of waved with her free hand, and he waved back.

She meandered the twisting walkway and went over to him, all those waiting, and greeting were creating sounds of excitement, laughter and chatter floated over her.

Her escort was a tall Latino looking, middle-aged gentleman who had a welcoming smile as she caught him looking her way.

"Are you waiting to take me to Tom?" she asked hesitantly.

"Yep, ma'am, that's me. Here, let me take your luggage."

The excitement within Moyra was almost beyond control.

"Do you have the money with you now or do you need to go to the bank? I can take you there if you need to exchange money?"

Moyra thought that all to be a bit sudden and even rude of him.

"Yes, I have the money, so no need for the bank. Do we have to go far now?"

"No, not too far," he answered.

The trip seemed to be taking rather a long time. *Will I ever get to Tom?*

"He has asked if I will entertain you at my place until he can come and meet up with you. Is that okay with you?"

"Yes, that's fine, I realise he is a busy man."

"That he is ma'am."

"Please call me Moyra, ma'am sounds so formal."

"Righty ho, ma'am. I will call you whatever you want to be called."

As he drove, Moyra took a furtive look at this rather handsome man sitting alongside her. He had dark brown, wavy hair down to his shirt collar. It was clean and she could smell the delicate aroma of an expensive men's aftershave. He had a bit of an Adonis look about him, swarthy, sun-tanned and slim.

"We are almost there now, hold tight as it's a bit of a sharp turn round here.

As they drove up to the door, she noticed how smart and well-kept everything seemed to be. The garden was laid out well, the borders filled with geraniums and roses, and hundreds of bushes all the same colour and design. *Clearly tastefully and designer arranged.*

The dwelling was a bungalow, a big one. As she attempted to get out of the car, Grant dashed over to her side and opened the door for her.

"Thank you, kind sir." *What a decent man he seems to be.*

That was until they got inside his home. "Well, do you have the money with you or not?"

Moyra was taken back a bit by the demanding way in which this was said.

"Yes, I have it, but I thought I was going to see Tom personally, and I'd give it to him."

"No, no, that's not the way it works. Ma'am you need to hand it to me. Tom hopes to be able to see you while you're over, but he is working on the latest production and may not be available for long," Grant said spuriously.

Moyra was at a loss as to what she should do. Of course, she wanted to make sure that the money she would hand over would be going to the person it was intended, but now alarm bells were ringing.

She had never felt as alone as she was doing right now. How sad that her desire for the friendship of a stranger had brought her to this juncture. She always thought of herself as an intelligent, trustworthy, and honest person and the thoughts she now experienced were anything but nice. Surely, she wouldn't have been sucked into something as dramatic and vacuous as she was beginning to imagine may be the case.

"Give the cash to me, and I will make sure Tom gets it. Then hang around for a bit and he may be able to see you. Stay here if you want, there's plenty of bedrooms, or I can take you to a hotel. What do you say, ma'am?"

"I think I would prefer that you take me back to Los Angeles and to the hotel, I have booked into."

"Okay, but what about the money?" He again demanded.

"I haven't made my mind up about that just yet. Will you drive me back to town, please?" she said, tentatively. She was afraid he may turn nasty and try to grab the money or possibly hurt her in some dramatic way.

"Yes, of course, but won't you have something to drink and maybe a bite before you go?"

She faltered for a second or two, wondering if he was being kind or trying to trap her. Her decision was to leave right away.

"Yes, yes, of course, I shall take you right away." He did not do so; instead he went into another room and made a telephone call that went on awhile.

She tried desperately straining her ears to try to catch what was being said, but in vain, as she thought he might not have been speaking in English. Moyra began to feel afraid and got up from where she'd sat in what she could only described as a tastefully decorated and well-designed lounge — delightfully furnished in golds and whites with a dash of red and cream-coloured cushions adorning the large settees. The inglenook type fireplace with logs in a large wicker basket almost adorned one side of the lengthy room. Strange, she should be considering furnishings in a place where fear was pervading her thoughts.

As she rose, she started pacing, something she always did when feeling nervous. She took her makeup bag from her portmanteau of a bag she'd brought with her. As she began to apply a fresh layer of the red lipstick she wore for the occasion along with a sprinkle of face powder from the compact, Grant returned. She hurriedly managed to get the makeup put away in the hope that he had not seen the activity.

He was smiling and said in a gentle voice. "Come on, lass; let's get you back to town."

Her mood brightened, and she felt more relaxed as they started to drive away in his limo type transport. She felt it appropriate to ask if the person he had spoken to on the phone was Tom.

"Yes, it was."

She could not help but think, *Then why on earth did he not speak to me? I have come over five thousand miles to meet up with him and he couldn't be bothered to talk to me.* "Well then, did you tell him I'd arrived and was with you at your home?"

"Of course, I did."

"Why did he not wish to talk to me then?"

"He is swamped, and he said he'd phone you when I let him know which hotel, you're staying in."

"Thanks for that and please let him know I want to see him personally to give him the money."

"I have already told him that, and that's the way you wish to do it."

They pulled up at a grand looking hotel, and Grant helped her with her cases up to the reception. A rather surly looking middle-aged woman stood there as if on guard. "Can I help you?" she said in a toxic voice

Grant said, "Yes, this lady is from England and needs a room for..." He turned to Moyra. "How long do you want the room booked for?"

"Five nights, I think."

The woman on guard said, "Could I have your details please? Name, address, and payment method."

"Not to worry about that, just put it in the name of Grant Pulanski." As he said that, he went to the right-side breast pocket of his jacket and pulled out a card that satisfied the guard on duty about its authenticity.

"Thank you, Grant."

A key was handed to him and he indicated to Moyra that she should follow him to the lift.

She hoped he didn't expect to be invited into the room; and he didn't. He unlocked the door, took the cases in and said to Moyra, "Well, will this do ma'am?"

"Will it do!" she exclaimed. "It's beautiful, lovely, thanks again and no problem at all."

Grant put his hand out toward hers, shook it, said goodbye and that he would be in touch and took his leave.

Wow, went through Moyra's mind. Thank goodness the room was being paid for by someone. Perhaps it was Tom himself. However, she thought that he did not have ready cash to splash about and the reason he'd asked her for money. She also was confused but pleased that Grant's attitude had improved and his manner became more pleasant.

She settled into her spacious room, which was gloriously decorated even smarter than the place she'd just left. The bedding and size of the bed were exquisite and the bathroom, half the size again of the bedroom.

She unpacked and lay on the bed thinking about the major error in judgement she may have been guilty of making. Had she been unwise in the thought of meeting up with her hero outweighing common sense? On deciding to make the most of what she was now experiencing and hoped that better things may be just around the corner.

She knew it was stupid to expect too much from Tom, and that she would be happy to see and talk with him again, even if only for a moment. She reckoned that if she kept her expectations low, anything more than that would be a bonus. She soon drifted to a peaceful sleep.

Chapter Thirteen

W hen she awoke, she could hardly believe the time, it was dark, and on looking at the watch laying on the bedside locker, it was midnight.

She could not believe how long she must have slept. She first entered the room at one in the afternoon and had not showered even though she knew she should after so long a journey.

Her first activity was to jump into the shower where she lingered a while. Feeling so much the better for it, she realised she had not eaten since leaving the airport, and then only eaten a small snack along with coffee before the plane landed.

She wandered over to the lift close to her room. The door soon opened, and she stepped in. It descended so fast it made her think she may fall. She landed in the reception area and asked a new female attendant the way to the dining room only to be told that it was closed and that she would need to order food from her room telephone to the kitchen.

"Oh, I haven't eaten for so long and I'm starving."

"You will need to do it from your room as they can tell you what is available. I can't. After all, ma'am, it's almost two-thirty in the morning."

"All right," Moyra announced and got back to her room as fast as she could. She ordered her food and said, "I hope it won't be long as I haven't eaten for ages."

"Right, ma'am. Be right up," came the reply. "We shall have it with you as soon as possible."

After the very tasty food was eaten, she felt so much better and thought she ought to take some exercise.

When she got to the front desk again, she was asked where she wanted to go.

"I don't really know; just thought I should get some fresh air and exercise!"

"It isn't safe to go out at this time of night, and alone, ma'am. I strongly advise you not to do so."
"Well, what shall I do then as I've been sleeping for hours and I'm wide awake and don't want to go back to bed, yet."

"If you don't have any reading matter, we have an excellent library, go down the corridor and turn left and you will see it clearly marked.
Moyra wandered down and was astounded to see the enormous number of books on display that included hardback, paperback, magazines, and newspapers spread out all over the tables.

She stayed there for an hour or two, feeling miffed that she was unable to leave the building, but thought it sensible to take the advice given.

Eventually, after flicking through all the newspapers and a couple of magazines, she decided to go up to her room and wait until the breakfast bar was opened.

She fell asleep again and awoke just in time to get washed, dressed and get down to the dining room before it closed. Here she enjoyed the most wonderful breakfast ever eaten.

Moyra had no idea that she would be offered so much food in American diners, never having visited one before. There was hot food, such as eggs, crispy bacon and grits. Cold food fresh fruit, pancakes with all the flavoured sauces you could imagine. Cereals, jams and every type of doughnut and pastries, one could only have dreamt about. She eagerly ate the food and was on her second helping, having first eaten the hot offered and now chomping her way through the cold. Back home, she never used to eat breakfast at all; just coffee and two tea biscuits, occasionally with an apple. As she was enjoying the last of this amazing breakfast, a young woman came over to her.

"There is a phone call for you ma'am. You are Mrs. Moyra French, I believe?"

"Yes, that's me, where shall I take it."

"Could you follow me, ma'am?"

She was led to the reception desk, handed the phone and found it was Grant the other end. "Morning Honey, and how are we this morning?" came a booming and happy voice.

"Well I am fine. Thanks, am I going to see Tom today?" At this comment, she noticed the receptionist look up from what was taking her interest on the desk in front of her.

"Well, that's what I'm calling about. I shall be over to pick you up later this morning. Does that suit you?"

"Yes, that's fine, I shall be waiting in the lobby."

She went back to finish her breakfast; she was still anxious not to miss out on anything and even went up a third time. This was so unlike Moyra who had never been a big eater. However, she had been ravenous from missing out on dinner the night before.

She went to her room, hung the few clothes she brought with her into the sliding door, magnificent walk-in clothes depository as it was named on the front of the glass door.

Then, she thought about going for a walk. She was on the third floor, walked down the stairs rather than taking the lift as the desire for exercise was becoming extremely strong.

She had two hours before Grant would be along to take her to see Tom and the butterflies in her stomach were having a party.

As she got to the door carousel at the hotel's front entrance, she walked down the steps after the doorman had doffed his hat in a greeting toward her. She was amazed to see how busy the street in front of her was. All the traffic racing around the blocks as though there was no time to waste. She heard nothing of the tremendous noise when in her bedroom.

It was then she realised that there were very few walkways in the city and that to get to the nearest park she was told she'd need to take a cab.

She was taken to the city centre, amazed and in awe by the wonderful shops filled with luxurious goodies of every famous worldwide brand known. *How can people ever afford to buy such incredibly expensive items was beyond her and certainly out of reach,* raced through her mind?

The immense amount of people shoving and pushing as she entered the stores made her feel ill, and she thought she might soon say hello to her breakfast. This had her running to the nearest convenience station. Fortunately, she managed to keep herself from vomiting, but decided she wasn't prepared for the scramble of it all; so, she left the store, wandered along a few more blocks. The constant business of it all got to her. She hailed a taxi and went back to the hotel where at least she would feel safe.

She wandered into the library after asking the bartender for a coffee. He told her to go and sit comfortably and that he would bring it to her.

"Will you be in the lounge, ma'am?" he inquired.

"No, I shall be in the library."

"A good choice, ma'am," he politely answered.

The time flew by and suddenly from behind where she sat, stood Grant tall and looking decidedly serious.

"Hi, are you okay?" said Moyra.

"Fraid not, Honey. Tom's in hospital, he got sick last night but said to get you to give me the money and that he would get to see you when he's better."

"Well, what happened to him, and how long will he be out of action?"

"Not sure to tell the truth. He had a grumbling appendix for a while and the doctor is threatening to take it out. So, who knows?"

"Well, I know I've had just about enough of this nonsense. I should have known something like this would happen. Can you tell me who paid for the hotel?"

"That was me; it was my card I used for you to stay here."

"Right, I shall spend tonight here and then I shall be back on the next plane I can get back to England. I shall pay you what you have paid only for the two nights and that will be an end to this fiasco."

Grant's face changed; he went a whiter shade of pale. "What about the money, he wants you to give me?"

"You surely don't think I'm going to give it to you, do you?"

"Well, yes, that's what you came here for, isn't it?"

"I did, but now I will not be doing so. As I said, I shall pay you for the stay here."

"Oh, I am sorry you feel this way. I was kinda looking forward to getting to know you better and showing you some of the sights of our beautiful city."

"No, I shan't be staying. You can tell Tom, or whoever he is that he is the biggest shit this side of the Atlantic."

"Ma'am, he really is ill; it's not a lie."

"I'm really am not interested anymore. How much do I owe you?"

"I'm not sure; I shall have to ask at reception." He went to find the price for the two nights. On his return, he told Moyra that it would be four hundred dollars and that they asked if everything was as you wished it to be. "If you don't believe me, go ask the girl. They wondered if you had a decent stay?"

"Right, here's your money. Now, please go as I have to re-arrange my flight."

Grant left with the most downtrodden look she had seen in a long time. It even had her feeling a little guilty for the way she had spoken to him.

It took her most of the rest of that day to organise the flight that would not be leaving until eight the next night.

She considered what the heck she would do for the whole day, deciding to return to the city. She was amazed to see the vast buildings that appeared to reach through the clouds as the sky was overcast and the clouds hung low. She again visited one of the famous stores the city offered and was surprised to find she was enjoying the hustle and bustle, this time. It took her mind away from the stupidity of which she had now convinced herself.

After an hour or two, she took a cab back to the hotel. It was six in the evening and she felt the pangs of hunger. She asked at the reception desk what time the restaurant would open.

"It's been open since four, ma'am; so, whenever you wish. It stays open until nine tonight."

Moyra went to her room, took a soak in the bath and then went down for supper.

She had only sat down about ten minutes when a friendly voice from behind her said, "Hello Moyra. Would you mind if I joined you?"

She panicked and thought it could be Tom. She was, however, wrong in that supposition and turned around to see Grant standing there and looking well and truly spruced up from earlier.

"I suppose so, after all, as far as I know, it's not you who has done me wrong or maybe it is? Anyway, it matters not one way or the other to me. I realise I have been the stupid one, and I'm off tomorrow so what the heck."

"Thank you, Moyra. I should like to buy you dinner as I'd like to hand you an olive leaf to apologise for all the trouble you've been caused and coming all the way over here for nothing."

"Yes, well, I've been a fool…" She proceeded to tell him the history of how the debacle began.

The evening passed quickly, and the dining room started to fill. They chatted on and off and Moyra could not help but notice how Grant kept staring at her. Eventually, she yawned and said, "Thank you for dinner; I shall accept your offer to pay for it."

"Now, what time do you have to be at the airport tomorrow?"

"It's five p.m."

"May I collect you and take you there?"

"No, thank you. I shall take a cab. You have done enough."

Grant put out his hand to wish her well and say goodbye. As he turned to leave her, he looked back and said, "You know, you are a lovely looking woman. May I leave you my contact details? So, if you ever come here again, I'd be delighted to meet up with you."

He handed her a scribbled note with his details of contact and then left.

Once again, guilt took over her feelings as she had not reciprocated the action. She also knew the way she'd treated him was not good, especially after he paid for the supper and had been pleasant and amenable company toward her throughout the evening. However, she thought he either had colluded with the said Tom, or it was Grant all along who was trying to defraud her and others more than likely. Thinking back to his expensive looking home, car and all the trimmings, that could well be the case.

She failed to sleep that night continually mulling over all that had happened since arriving in America. Not settling, she got out of bed and read from her Kindle Fire and thought that might send her off. But no! She rose, had breakfast, packed her few bits and pieces. It was then that a sudden idea came to mind. *Why don't I go and try to find out where Tom lives in the morning? Maybe call him and say something along the lines of Guess who. Then, I may get to see him once again.*

She knew she was in the city where he had a home. She went to the Traveller's Advice Booth and asked if they knew where he lived. They told her that he had a home in Beverly Hills, but that it was highly unlikely he would be there.

"Is there any way I could go up there and see for myself?"

"Yes, a bus tour takes tourists up into the Hills and they point out places that the rich and famous live, ma'am. However, the houses are extremely well protected, and visitors are seriously frowned upon. They will tell you that on the bus."

Thanking the staff for their help, she booked her ticket right away and waited.

The tour started at eleven a.m. and was for one and a half hours.

She didn't have too long to wait and got talking to another lady waiting for the same tour who was fascinated that she was English and asked about the Royal family.

She cued along a snaking line of holidaymakers, dressed in shorts and T-shirts all laughing and making conversations with one another. She took her seat and handed her ticket to the driver, a man anxious to make sure that everyone had paid the correct price, then off they went.

She felt happy that she would at least see where Tom lived, maybe only once while on a tour, but at least it was where he had been present some time or another. She also enjoyed the trip except for the driver who gave a running commentary of the high spots, most of which she failed to understand as his accent was a thick southern American drool.

She did, however, clearly hear him say, "And this folks, this is the house that's owned by Tom Ursuline; the celebrity."

Not much further up the road, the bus stopped allowing passengers to get out for photoshoots.

"Don't be more than ten minutes as we need to carry on to the top."

She was overwhelmed by the feeling that she thought she'd make a run for it and see if she could get into the house.

She managed to sneak away and go up to the gate where an intercom was in use. She pushed the bell and was surprised when someone answered it.

"Can I help you," a voice said quietly.

"Good morning, my name is Moyra French and I'm here from England to see Mr. Ursuline." She was even more surprised when the gates began to open for her.

Slowly and cautiously, she walked through and a short way along the drive, she saw a young woman coming toward her.

They greeted one another, and the host said to Moyra, "I am sorry, but he is not here. He is rarely here, in fact. I am the head housekeeper and keep the place running when he's away. Was he expecting you?"

"No, he wasn't expecting me. I met him a while back in England and was passing and took a chance that he might home. Thank you so much for letting me see his home this close. I'm on the tourist bus and you can't see how beautiful it is from there. Thank you again; now I must go and catch the bus. Mora extended her hand to shake one of Tom's head housekeeper. Would you be kind enough to let him know, that is when you see him, that Moyra French popped in. I don't suppose for one moment that he will remember me."

"Don't be too sure of that; he has an amazing memory. I hope you have a smooth trip back to England!"

"Thank you again. Goodbye."

Moyra left Tom's beautiful home in all its splendour whitewashed walls with pale green paintwork. At the main doorway, stood a huge trellis covered in vines and a variety of roses.

She missed the bus, as she suspected would happen and wondered what on earth to do. She was way away from Los Angeles and thought she'd better call a cab, not knowing any of the numbers to be able to do so. She went back to Tom's front gate and rang the bell.

"I am so sorry to ask this, but I need to call a cab as I've missed the bus and I don't know any numbers to call them. Would you mind doing that for me?"

"Yes, of course, I will."

Within around five minutes, the cab arrived and returned her to the hotel. She was charged a small fortune for the forty-minute ride.

Moyra marvelled at the fact that she had seen inside the gate of Tom's home and the kindness shown by his housekeeper. She would always have that memory from her trip to California; even if it had not turned out the way she hoped.

She readied herself for the flight and took a cab to the airport where she waited the required three hours. To pass the time, she bought three cups of coffee and ate a bar of chocolate. The taste reminded her of the old cooking chocolate she used to have in the U.K. back in the sixties. However, as it was the first thing she ate since her gargantuan breakfast, she was grateful.

Chapter Fourteen

On the flight back home, she thought about all that had happened on the four-day trip, counting the two flights. *How could I have been such a fool as to have believed that the person asking for money was the celebrity I met in the past? asking for money was the celebrity I met in the past?* Whatever possessed her to be that stupid and be taken in by the kind and loving words almost unheard in her life since the death of her mother, she deduced that loneliness was the reason she'd fallen for it all.

Still, she had had some good come from it all. First, there was Grant, a pleasant enough and most handsome individual, with a lovely body and he, had bought her dinner and offered to help in other ways.

It had not turned out as bad as it could have. Anything could have happened. She could have been kidnapped or even killed for the money. She had been lucky.

Then, the closeness to the home of her heart's desire.

She still had her three thousand pounds, and she had a short holiday.

After arriving back home, those who knew she went to America questioned her being away for such a short time.

She gave all manner of excuses including her dislike for the place and being alone never once letting on about the real reason for her visit.

She knew that her life must now become more fulfilled, and although she didn't trust the internet for making relationships, she hadn't ruled out perhaps trying to find a companion from there in the future.

She would also try to get a few more hours at her workplace. She didn't think that would be difficult as they always seemed to need help in some form or other. The farm, after all, was an ever-expanding enterprise.

The thought of getting in contact with Grant gave her sleepless nights, but she resisted the temptation. She made sure those thoughts didn't hang around for long. However, she could not summon up the courage to dismiss the possibility of another, and a maybe longer trip across the pond one day.

After almost a month after her return home, she heard a knock on her door. It was a delivery from the States and she received a hamper of numerous goodies and on the card. She opened and read his message.

To Dear Moyra, so sorry I was not at home. Love Tom.

The end.

About the Author

Joy is a published author of several novels, short stories and has articles published in magazines. She spent a lifetime as a trained nurse before becoming a writer. Her first novel, "Figs, Vines and Roses," tells of a moving tale of love and loss at the turn of the nineteenth century. Her nursing background gave her the inspiration for the last book, "Times Pendulum Swings Again," a hospital romance that goes badly wrong. Her novel, "Strawberry Moon," is set in the Dordogne, France and tells of a young man's murder. "The Liberty Bodice," is set in 1922 United Kingdom. When not writing, Joy works as a voice-over artist. She also spends time with her large family, and the little ones affectionately knowing her as Nanny G.

ALL BOOKS AVAILABLE ON AMAZON